"*A Necessary Chaos* is a modern epic o
lovers with horrifically awesome magic and immaculate vibes. *This Is How You Lose The Time War* meets Rage Against the Machine."
—Kate Elliott, author of *Unconquerable Sun* and *The Servant Mage*

"*A Necessary Chaos* is the gay 'spy versus spy' story that I've been waiting for. Short and sharp, this is a powerful jab of a novella: it'll leave you dazed and dizzy and a little bit in love."
—C.L. Clark, author of *The Unbroken* and *The Faithless*

"Horny and heartbreaking, exhilarating and emotional, *A Necessary Chaos* is jam-packed with brilliant worldbuilding and stunning character work—heralding the arrival of a major new talent on the SF/F/H scene."
—Sam J. Miller, author of *Blackfish City* and *Boys, Beasts and Men*

"Proudly anti-imperialist and unapologetically queer, *A Necessary Chaos* is a sensual action-packed fantasy that doesn't shy away from feelings. Amor vincit omnia—even empires."
—Francesca Tacchi, author of *Let the Mountains Be My Grave*

"I couldn't put *A Necessary Chaos* down. There's sexiness, romance, action and intrigue; every page brings more surprises. A very fun read."
—Eboni Dunbar, author of *Stone and Steel*

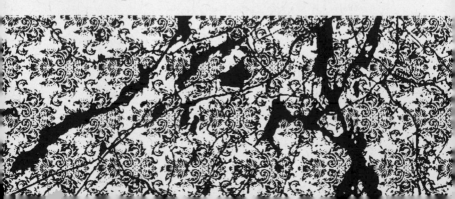

**Neon Hemlock Press**
www.neonhemlock.com
@neonhemlock

© 2023 Brent Lambert

**A Necessary Chaos**
**Brent Lambert**

**Cover Illustration** by Cathy Kwan
**Cover Design and Layout** by dave ring
**Interior Illustrations** by Matthew Spencer
**Interior Design and Layout** by dave ring
**Edited** by dave ring

**Print ISBN-13:** 978-1-952086-46-5
**Ebook ISBN-13:** 978-1-952086-47-2

Brent Lambert
**A NECESSARY CHAOS**

*Neon Hemlock Press*

# A
# Necessary
# Chaos

BY BRENT LAMBERT

*To that teenage boy who never thought he'd find this life,
thank you for holding on. And for my family and friends that may not
have always understood my imagination, but loved it anyway.*

# THE CORRIN ISLANDS — LAPIS BEACH

**P**RECISE JUDGMENT WAS a prerequisite for Vade's work and he could say without a doubt that nobody had an ass like Althus. Vade watched his assignment, his lover, his…something he didn't have the courage to name yet, walk towards the pristine ocean completely naked. Their bodies were the most honest thing between them. And Althus's was a masterpiece to behold. Wide shoulders, smooth light brown skin, and ample cheeks Vade never got enough of cupping his hands around.

Coming to Lapis Beach had been Althus's idea. Vade had to laugh at all the ways Althus tried to disarm him over the course of their sporadic but long-lived, staged romance. They linked up four or five times a year at vacation spots in sensual, eclectic locations. This was meet-up number…twenty? Twenty-two? Keeping track of anything was hard when he watched Althus. There were people you fucked and people who fucked you. Althus fell firmly in the latter.

Desiree, his commander, would kill him for the thought. Althus was a target. A rebel to be observed, mined for information, and eliminated one day for the greater security of the world. It was cold analysis and should have been easy after fifteen years of being a Whisper. Finding the quietest way to kill someone, discovering the slightest stroke to end a so-called social movement and the smallest push to topple uncooperative nations had been his sworn duty. Was *still* his sworn duty, but Althus left him confused. The man's smile and his grip, sowed doubts.

Vade walked to the water, wrapped his arms around Althus's chest, and pressed his body against his lover's muscular curves. This wasn't confusion. This felt right. Them alone and the world too far away for him to give a damn about any of its expectations. Vade knew he should have told his superiors he was compromised years ago, but he refused to give up these moments.

Guilt poked at him, torn between duty and…he wouldn't name it.

"How'd you know I wasn't some deranged killer sneaking up on you?" Vade asked playfully. The beach horizon marched towards eventide, giving them a sun caught between orange and purple.

"No one comes to a place this beautiful to start shit," Althus laughed, leaning his head gently back against Vade's shoulder. "And besides, I know your footsteps. I know your breathing. I know your heartbeat."

"Ha! What heart? I am strictly a man of business." Vade traced his fingers along Althus's bicep, wondering if he touched the dragon tattoo magic kept hidden. The tattoo marking Althus as part of the Phantom Dragon, sanctimonious rebels entirely sure that the chaos they sowed would bring about a better world.

"Please! You melt every time a kid smiles at you."

Althus wasn't wrong. Vade felt momentarily exposed, but knew how to flip it back. "Your smile does that too.

Every. Single. Time."

"Don't get used to it. I don't like you that much."

The way they held each other conveyed the exact opposite.

Vade squeezed tighter. "I'm glad you decided on this place. I thought Iluma was beautiful, but holy shit this water is damn near translucent."

"We should stay the night and watch the glow eels dancing in the waves."

Vade kept his composure but he saw the dig for what it was. The glow eels circling around the Corrin Islands were a byproduct of magical experimentation conducted by the Compact thirty years ago. Maybe most people would see them as unexpected beauty arising from the need for progress, but not Althus. And as much as they talked around their feelings, they talked around their politics too. Vade held no illusions. He knew Althus was spying on him too. Their cross purposes had always been clear to one another.

Vade took his own jab. "The glow eels are a real marvel. There's too many people who don't appreciate them."

Though regrettable, the military experiments conducted were critical towards ending the twelve-year long civil war in the Xiogo Coast. Maintaining the delicate balance in the world required strength.

Vade could admit it wasn't a perfect arrangement. But the world wasn't made for perfect. The best you could hope for was something lasting, and even that was a gamble. Althus and the Phantom Dragons would tear the serenity of the world apart to sate their over bloated, unrealistic sense of justice. He admired their conviction and their willingness to stand against forces so much larger than themselves, but the path of destruction those beliefs paved infuriated him.

"I've heard the locals learned to make a pretty interesting meal out of them," Althus said. "We could order it at dinner tonight."

It was a concession. Vade traced a finger down Althus's abs and smiled when the other man shivered a bit. It felt good knowing his touch could still evoke that response.

"I can think of a few other meals I'd rather try first." Vade nibbled a bit on Althus's ear. "Unless business is going to have you tied up tomorrow?"

This was their lie. They told each other they were international businessmen. Not assassin and rebel. Not enemies.

"Business is one of those things I can always re-arrange. What'd you have in mind?"

Before Vade could give a proper answer, a group of Corrin Island locals swept over a sand dune. They danced to the rhythm of drums and sparkling, golden maracas, just as naked as they were. Their arrival put a heart-crushingly large grin on Althus's face. He gave Vade a brief wink and joined their dancing. That was how it was on the Corrin Islands: happiness overflowed with soul-soothing music, fish seared to perfection, and perfect nights on the beach. Vade watched Althus take an elderly woman into his arms—she taught Althus a few steps and soon he was bouncing off his heels like they were.

Vade simply observed, making sure none were using their instruments to conceal weapons. The Corrin Islands might be joyous, but they still had their rebel elements. Yesterday, Vade had inspected an underground site not too far from this very beach where the Amos-Morbine Compact carried out interrogations of high level targets. Vade had wondered more than once since arriving if Althus was aware of it.

That was the constant ebb and flow between them. Vade trying to figure out Althus's true motives in their every interaction and Althus doing the same. At least, he assumed that to be the case. What other reason could a rebel have to not just kill him outright? There was so much else Vade knew about Althus, but it would all be deemed superficial and unimportant by his superiors.

Vade knew Althus was allergic to cats and could barely breathe around them. He knew Althus laughed at his own jokes so vigorously he pulled everyone into laughter with him. And he knew Althus loved to dance. The first time Vade let his guard down around Althus— in a sweaty, backwater club tucked into the isolated, white shrubbery-covered mountains of Guerrado, where the drinks were strong and the people came to party without pretension—Vade remembered thinking Althus moved his hips like the rhythm was made just for him. Vade almost forgot he was a Whisper that night, dancing up against him. It was then he knew he wasn't going to shake Althus loose.

Watching Althus move with abandon on a nude beach was a hell of a turn on. He enjoyed this snippet of unfiltered, unmasked happiness. Who knew what life might be if they could have this moment forever, but like water crashing against sandcastles on the beach, nothing happy between them would ever last.

Eventually, the locals tired of Althus's boundless energy and moved on. "I think you exhausted them," Vade teased when Althus came back.

Althus put his hands on his knees and laughed. "They had at least ten more rounds in them. It's just late is all."

"Late, huh?" Vade looked him square in the eye and bit his bottom lip. "Probably not as many people here."

"Say less." Althus slid into his arms, grabbing the back of Vade's neck to bring warm mouths together.

This was how it was with them. Electric. Unquenchable.

Vade gripped Althus's hips and pulled him closer as they made out. His body was warm and flecked with sand. Tracing Althus's body felt like caressing a piece of art. Vade knew exactly where to touch him. A press against his lower back made Althus arch and like the steps of a memorized dance, Vade ran his tongue against his lover's neck.

Their love-making was no longer furious, lustful grabs.
They had spent enough time exploring each other to
treat it like a long road trip, finding beauty in each stop
along the way. In the beginning, Vade hated himself
for wanting Althus so bad, for letting him distract from
his mission. But now, all he ever looked forward to were
these moments where they came together like a cosmic
alignment.

The friction, sand against skin, turned him on even
more. There always came a point in their love-making
when his body demanded more. Vade reached under
Althus's thighs and hoisted him up to his waist.

Althus laughed, feeling Vade's stiffness against him.
"You think you'll be able to keep me up the whole time?"

"I've bounced you off worse places." Althus had been
joking, but the exchange filled Vade with a sudden need.
They both moaned as Vade entered him, right there on
the beach. Vade didn't care. The thought of being caught
made his strokes faster, until the sound of hips slapping
against ass became louder than the surf. Althus groaned
against his chest and dug his fingers harder into Vade's
shoulders. Anyone stupid enough to try and arrest them
would regret it. Vade was the invisible scalpel of a gigantic
empire, and this moment was his work (he kept hoping if
he said it enough times he'd believe it was only that).

As he came, Vade heard another voice, masculine and
insidious, roaring within his mind: *Take him. Consume him.
Make him yours.*

For as long as he'd known Althus, since the first time
they came together, he'd heard this voice in his mind.
Maybe he should be more frightened, but he didn't know
how to explain it and the words left Vade feeling charged.
He *wanted* to make Althus his. And if he reported the voice
to his superiors, they would pull him off this mission. He'd
get thrown into a lab for them to poke and prod. Vade
had made too much progress for that be his end.

"That was fun," Althus said after, laughing while fighting for breath. "Walking back to the hotel might be a little rough though."

Vade, emboldened by the voice, leaned in for another possessive kiss and gripped Althus's hard-on. "Taking care of this will buy us some time. I could keep kissing you."

Althus would have no idea that Vade's last words—"I could keep kissing you"— were something else in Two-Voice, the magical language practiced by Whispers like himself. Only those who could speak it could understand it. To everyone else, it sounded like innocuous phrases, normal and out of place alike. He'd just returned some of the energy Althus must have lost from the dancing. Maybe enough that he'd change his mind about—

"Naw. It's getting late. Let's just get back to the hotel." Althus rubbed Vade's ear between his fingers.

Vade swept his target up in his arms. "I'll carry you."

And he would figure out the voice. He'd make this all work somehow.

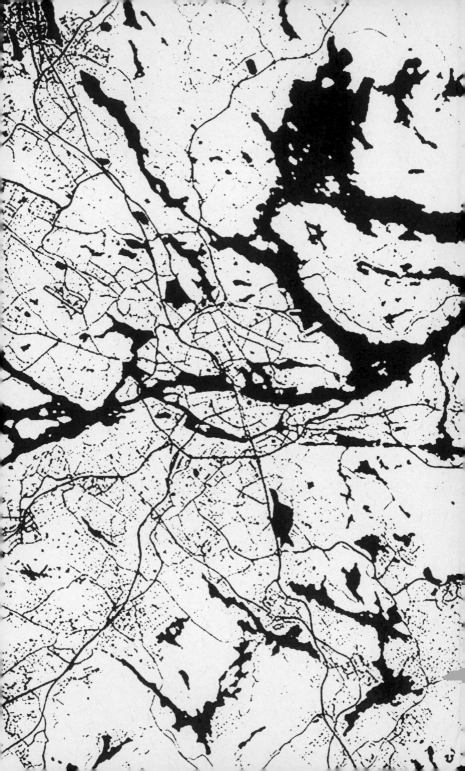

# TASHEDIN CITY

ALTHUS COULDN'T EXPLAIN it, but every time he got with Vade it felt like the best sex he'd ever had. It left him feeling unworldly good and, worse, he couldn't tell anyone about it. This man worked for the worst of the three empires. Vade was a killer through and through. His comrades hunted down activists who wanted freedom. He played a role in the destruction of a better world. But oh man could he fuck!

He told himself that was the only reason he felt the way he did. This bliss was physical pleasure—the heat of their bodies intertwined—and nothing more. It had nothing to do with how expertly Vade disarmed people with a few kind words and a wink. It wasn't how perfectly he walked the tightrope of vanity and confidence, never acknowledging the eyes lusting for him, never letting an ego grow from them. No, Althus stayed with Vade because he had a mission: use him to glean information from the Amos-Morbine Compact so the Phantom Dragons could keep chipping away at the voracious power of the empires.

After that brief idyllic stay in the Corrin Islands, they separated like they always did, both of them returning to jobs that didn't exist. Althus did everything he could to pretend the ache in his chest wasn't there, spending the boat ride back to the port city of Tashedin—another unwilling territory of the Amos-Morbine Compact— drinking shots passed to him by a patient bartender. The boat was fancier than his usual transport—he had to keep up his cover in case someone tailed him, even though he was pretty sure Vade already knew exactly who he was.

He sat beside two drunk older women, a couple judging by their amethyst wedding bracelets, discussing the possibility of magic overuse tearing down the barriers between dimensions and unleashing a whole host of monsters on the world. One threw up her hands with great gusto, describing manticores swallowing children and dragons burning through the skies once again. The woman's enthusiasm reminded him of Vade when he talked about the history of candies across the world.

Althus's people would never forgive him if they knew about all the things he admired—the kindness, compassion and integrity—in his imperial agent. He could never tell them. The Phantom Dragons were loyal to each other, but even loyalty had limits. It'd be like telling a stabbing victim he'd fallen in love with the knife that ripped them open. As he swished around his last shot, Althus imagined running away from these... noble intentions to break the world. What would a mutual confession look like with Vade? They'd be on the rooftop of a nightclub, maybe in the Enoch Consortius, with drums kicking, people dancing close, blood vultures circling as the light attracted them, with just a smattering of rain. Vade would look at him, lips parted, and pull his wet body in close. They'd admit to the thrill of openly lying to each other. How the game was almost as hot as the sex. And then they'd both confess to wanting more...

Althus groaned and threw back the last shot, washing away this foolish imagined rendezvous. They'd arrived. Tashedin wasn't as romantic a city as the one he just envisioned and it was best navigated by motorbike. Althus paid for one of the quick rentals at the shops lining the port and took off towards his safe house. One of the first things the Phantom Dragons had taught him was the need to keep moving. A single location inevitably become a trap, and they refused to become the latest counter-imperial group to be wiped out by an empire's special agents. To survive, they had to fly and buzz around the gigantic empires, moving fast enough that they couldn't be swatted. So the Phantom Dragons kept safe houses scattered throughout the globe, places they could retreat to after each operation. The Phantom Dragons had been busy of late: they'd bombed an illegal pharmaceutical testing site in the Enoch Consortius, prevented the Compact's arrest of a major dissident leader from the Coati Legion, and burned a crop of experimental grain the Phobeta Courts would have used to destabilize the Southern agriculture market. But too much success was an easy way to gain the undivided attention of the empires, so it was time to lay low.

Althus zipped through the traffic on the city's main highway, barely avoiding getting knocked clean off his motorbike by a few careless drivers. The usual custom in Tashedin was to exchange some angry words, but he was still too stuck on Vade to play along. Why did leaving that man feel like coming down? He used to write this off as just an erotic rush from fucking with forbidden fruit. But there was something deeper there and when he thought too much about why, it filled Althus with shame.

Whispers like Vade were among the greatest defenders of a broken status quo and here he was getting an anxious stomach at the thought of one.

"Fucking stupid," he growled, pulling into the parking lot across the street from the raggedy, run-down apartment building that held his safe house. In the morning, he'd return the motorbike and catch a flight out of Tashedin. Maybe a good night's sleep would clear his head.

The apartment building entrance was a rounded arch of graffitied gray stone, marked by, Althus assumed, a few of the local gangs. One of the tags read in large, extravagant letters: FUCK MAGGICTS! CHESYRAH FOREVER!

Good ol' *maggict*. A perfect blend of magic, maggot and addict. A proclamation, insult, and accusation all in one. The tag was written in the sharp, harsh characters of Ptar—the language of the Amos-Morbine Compact. Althus approved. There was a dark irony in using the language of your oppressor to insult them.

Althus balled his fingers into a fist and flared them out to mimic an explosion. Chesyrah was the closest to a saint the Phantom Dragons had. Magic was what set the world on this path, where satisfying greed and seeking power knew no end. The empires existed because they had gained access to three terrifying dimensions and pulled horror after horror from them. Althus would never have been forced to become a child soldier if not for magic. Tashedin would still be an independent city.

A rundown courtyard in the middle of the building might have once made the place look majestic. Now the fountain was covered in mold, the water sickly in color and its orange tiles long overdue for a good pressure washing. A set of rickety, rusty stairs to the right of the courtyard took him to apartment number 10.

He hadn't been to this one in over a year, and by the looks of it, neither had the others. Tashedin wasn't exactly a tourist destination and its citizenry had long ago decided survival was enough. Any anger they had at the larger world, they mostly turned on each other. It broke his heart to see a people so defeated, but the Phantom Dragons had to focus on those willing to fight.

He waved dust out of his face as he stepped into the apartment. Before he took another step, he called on his magical talent. "Opix endu." His eyes closed as they became unreasonably heavy, but only until the feeling of cold iron grazing his fingertips snapped him back to attention.

The apartment glowed silver for a moment until the light tinkled away like broken glass. Althus relaxed; it would have been golden if someone had infiltrated the space. Anyone in the vicinity would have just heard him say, "This place could use a maid." That was the danger of Two-Voice. Your every word could carry magic with it and only someone else who also spoke Two-Voice would ever know—one day Vade would learn about Althus's Two-Voice, but luckily there was no indication of that yet.

Your drink in a nightclub could be made poison and the whole time you thought they were just complimenting your fit. They could be asking for a kiss and turning your intestines to stone. Deception was at the root of Two-Voice. Maybe that was why he and Vade were such a perfect fit.

The only couch in the place was a dingy brown two-seater. He lifted up a corner and withdrew a small, white wooden box. The Phantom Dragons had also taught him to never be too secretive about the things you didn't want people to find. Hide openly in the undesired places of the world and you could stay a step ahead of the empires. That's what made Althus hold out hope for Vade. He didn't seem to regard the whole world as a dirty place only allowed to exist by the grace of his government. And yet how could someone know all the ways his government had harmed the world and choose to serve them anyway?

It was a contradiction that Althus didn't want to spend too much time examining.

He sat down with the box on the floor, messing up the very expensive pants he'd brought to the Corrin Islands.

Not that he should care. Attaching value beyond necessity to material things was disastrous for the soul, Akjo always said. One of the principles the Phantom Dragons stood by was that the wanton desire for material things—and people were just another form of material—stood right at the heart of the empires' power.

Althus couldn't argue. The Amos-Morbine Compact even codified it into their military doctrine: *Aggressive defense and benevolent possession at all times.* They had the audacity to call it a compassionate policy. As if wanting to possess a thing entirely could ever be benevolent. But that was part of the delusion. Althus had read the propaganda: all three empires were convinced that their unchecked conquest, secured with magic's terrible strength, was the best means of keeping the world safe.

The Phantom Dragons used a network of enchanted boxes as their primary means of communicating information. Any of them could drop in a letter and copies of it would appear in however many of the other boxes they needed to. He sat a hand atop the box and summoned Two-Voice again. The box glowed silver.

Inside the box was a small journal with an unassuming brown leather cover, kept closed by a small string of twine. Althus used Two-Voice to move the journal from safe house to safe house, wherever another box was located. After each encounter with Vade, he meticulously wrote down his observations.

Small moments from their trysts often provided vital details that saved lives. Once, Vade tried to hide the fact that he was sick and hurled off a hotel balcony in the process. When Althus investigated, he learned not only that the people below weren't thrilled, but by asking questions about the unusually sweet odor of the vomit, how Vade had acquired a disease local to the Caseen Slopes. And with that knowledge, the Phantom Dragons were able to work with insurgents there to locate a Compact research site.

Another time, Vade had done his best to conceal a leg wound. No one would have noticed his limp but Althus, and when they fucked that night, he climbed on top, with his back to Vade, and got a good long look. From the shape of the wound, he determined it had come from a knife used by scalegrass collectors in the Hamarind provinces, a people that had been resisting the power of the empires for decades. Althus convinced the other Phantom Dragons to reallocate their resources and saved the lives of countless vital culture-workers in that region.

It was the little details that mattered. Althus smiled, no longer suffocated by his doubts.

"You're not around your little Whisper anymore. You're home. Show your true colors."

Althus jumped to his feet but slid back to cool calm as he recognized the voice. As a child soldier, his superior used to beat him every time he flinched until he learned to remain in control. The source of this training was atrocious but it had kept him from making many dumb decisions since then. Going to go to blows with one of his fellow Phantom Dragons would have been unpleasant.

"You could let me know if you plan on tagging me next time." Althus let his tattoo come to life: a long, smoky black dragon encircling his right arm.

Karmola laughed, rich and full of bass, as she leaned against the window. Her own tattoo sat right on her collarbone and traveled up her neck in white ink instead of black. "Wasn't tagging you, love. But I wanted to talk in person rather than waiting till you got my next communique."

Karmola had a tall, domineering presence with a beauty that refused to be tamed by the world. Dark, majestic skin and boundless black hair full of coils. Her smile carried a feral quality, oscillating between making him feel like she would hide a body for him or make him the one she's hiding. Althus had to admit, either option thrilled him. Karmola had been rattling the cages of empires for years. She'd survived as long as she had by being relentlessly precise in her choices. And she wasn't the type to do anything on a whim. "Okay, lay it on me."

"It's about the woman holding your pet Whisper's leash."

Althus stiffened but hoped she didn't notice. "He just mentioned something about needing a pair of gloves for his next trip. Said he'd pick them up from a store called Warm Delights. It's located out of Byris."

"Where the Legion are holed up."

Althus nodded. "Could be a load of crap, but I think the Whispers are going to move against the Coati again."

Karmola whistled. "I'll channel it through the Ten Ocelots. They have a direct connect with the Coati. Your work with the Whisper hasn't gone unnoticed. But that's what I want to talk to you about. It's time to decide how we're moving beyond it."

"Beyond it how?"

"More than just Desiree's usual plans are on the table right now. Access to the Onyx Cabin is about to be in play here."

Desiree Halmis, the creator of the Whispers, was one of the vilest players operating in any of the major empires. She was a butcher, cold and efficient, cursed by suits in both the halls of the Enoch Consortius and the Phobeta Courts, and a huge part of how the Amos-Morbine Compact marched towards supremacy. In the decade since she'd taken command, Whispers had hunted down no less than fifty rebel groups and dissident organizations around the world.

The Onyx Cabin was meant to be one of the most well-guarded facilities in the world, and believed to contain copies of every shred of Two-Voice research that Desiree had ever conducted, with everything from cutting edge research to fragments of spells that could potentially destabilize entire continents. If it even existed—anyone who tried to get close to it was never heard from again.

While Althus had spent years surveilling Vade, Karmola had spent just as long looking for a way to crack the Onyx Cabin wide open.

Althus hated Desiree. Death was her orchestra and she its maestro. He'd convinced himself that Vade's soul had been mangled by this woman's brutal training that burned out all compassion and empathy. The Whispers were her personal hounds of war. Vade answered to her and no one else. She was a fucking maggict, if anyone was. The Phantom Dragons knew that her need to cultivate power had taken her down dark paths. Rumors abound about her research involving the torture dimension and what lied in it. Finding a way into the Onyx Cabin could expose all those crimes.

"You found it, didn't you? How do we get in?"

"It's real. I'm sure of it now. The security system she has in place for it is maddeningly singular and makes me question the woman's sanity, but yes; I found a way in. There's a password that changes with each new assignment, and a new Whisper is assigned to it at unusual intervals. Learning the password has proven difficult, but the next Whisper in the rotation…"

Althus took a deep breath. "It's Vade, isn't it?"

Karmola leaned forward. "So now I have to ask; do you think you can pull the password out of him?"

Althus bit his bottom lip. He wanted to say yes but he'd be lying. The man's integrity would never let him betray the empire he'd sworn himself to. "Even if we tortured him, I don't think he'd give it up. But maybe I could get it with Two-Voice." Althus had discovered a phrase to to speak with the recently dead—it was elegant, if brutal. An extreme measure. But Althus had always known that eventually Vade's life might be forfeit in this struggle.

"I'm not dumb, Althus. You've been assigned to this target for a long time. I know the attachments that long-term missions can create. I'll do it."

It was tempting, but Karmola, no matter how many times she'd tried, couldn't pronounce the phrase. And it only worked on a fresh corpse, so Althus had to be there. He shook his head. "No. I'm the only one who can do it."

He wouldn't let Karmola see the conflict in his heart— there shouldn't *be* any conflict. It had been a masterclass in bad choices to view Vade as anything more than a task. Althus knew that. Vade was a killer. There was a long trail of evidence indicating just that. Fuck. But the pieces were coming together for him. Karmola *knew* she wasn't the right person for this job. Which meant… "You already put this to the vote, didn't you? And you're here to make sure I vote for whatever your plan is."

Karmola shrugged. "You know how we do things. Majority or nothing. And Sajime is being a little bitch about it."

"The vote's going to be that close huh?"

Her voice softened. "I wouldn't be out here if it wasn't important."

Althus balled up his fists. "So? What's the plan?"

"You lure Vade into your honey trap. I kill him. You pull the password. We access the Onyx Cabin and sweep it before Desiree realizes her precious hound is dead."

"But the others think taking out a Whisper right now isn't a good play, don't they? There's been too many other players getting wiped off the board lately. If we keep pushing, the empires won't think we're just annoyances anymore."

"More or less. But it's a clear sign our efforts are working. This is when we should press, not retreat."

"Sajime will be pissed if she finds out you were trying to manipulate the vote."

"Please. She expects no less."

His box started to shake behind him, sending him into a cold sweat, knowing there was a slip in there asking for his vote. He still cared about Vade, and Karmola had all but called him out on it. It was a testament to their friendship that her hunches hadn't made it around to the rest of the Phantom Dragons. Besides, she was right. And now he needed to prove her wrong.

"I'll vote for your plan. On one condition." Althus forced as much fearsome determination into his voice as he could muster. "I do this alone. If I don't make it, the Phantom Dragons need someone alive who can still use Two-Voice."

Karmola didn't try to hide her victorious smirk. "You're made for this, Althus. You always have been."

# THE HALMIS ESTATE — INSINU ISLAND

**D**ESIREE'S ESTATE WAS gigantic. Vade could never get used to it. His life as a Whisper before the assignment to Althus saw him sequestered to average hotel rooms, dirty rentals, and the small homes of other agents trying to live unassuming lives. He got to be more flashy now, yes, but the kind of wealth on display at Desiree's home was both foreign and a source of pride for him. This was what the empire could provide to its citizens and to the world if they would only let it.

That was why Vade served the Amos-Morbine Compact—for the day when the world no longer needed people like him. When the empires recognized their superior culture and yielded. Then the real work of building a better world could begin, absent the division at the heart of so many of their woes. If he and the other Whispers could remove that, the world could become something magnificent.

He knew his sister would be proud of him for staying the course. And when he found her…he pushed that image aside. Now wasn't the time.

The whole estate was an architectural testament to the power and history of the Amos-Morbine Compact. The gate surrounding the compound was an elaborate iron and black shadow box fence. The lumber came from the Twisted Forest of the Enoch Consortius. The blue and yellow gems in the center of each panel could only have come from mines under the protective gaze of the Phobeta Courts, a rival empire. It was both insult and praise: Desiree made it clear she could take what she wanted from her enemies, but that she could still find value in their works. Vade respected her for it.

Maybe that's all he was doing with Althus. Recognizing the beauty and power in a foe. After all, the namesake of his rebel group drew its inspiration from such a potent combination. Phantom dragons were a thing of ancient history, deadly and rare, but always respected. Lies and legends more than life but still—aside from all its political baggage, the name was fitting for Althus.

Fluted stone columns flanked the entrance, a manticore swallowing a sword etched into the stone at the top of each one. At the base of the columns, etched and lacquered with gold, were the words best exemplifying the moral character of the Compact: *Destiny is a burden only the great can bear.*

Price and purpose. It was a declaration every citizen of the Compact held to. But beneath that saying at the heart of their unified imperial identity, Whispers read instead a Two-Voice phrase: *Telo rrinada ora awlu aida tsaw.*

They were the first words ever spoken by D.L. Halmis, Desiree's great-grandparent, when they came back from the torture dimension. D.L. had been the Compact scientist who discovered and first traversed the torture dimension, encountering its never-ending landscape of screams and pain long enough to tell about it.

How someone was able to distill magic from that landscape was one of history's greatest questions.

Halmis's discovery sparked a global scramble to find other sources of magic. The only powers to succeed were the Enoch Consortius and the Phobeta Courts, who discovered the cancer and war dimensions respectively, bringing Blacknails and Paleskins into the world. Soon it became a magical arms race between those three world powers.

The mission of the Amos-Morbine Compact was a noble one, but that did not mean everyone working towards its ultimate goal was. Linguistic aptitude came into play with everyone who used Two-Voice. Some Whispers could never pronounce certain words right and thus had numerous effects cut off from them. Others just couldn't learn to ever say particular words at all, their minds wouldn't let them. Vade was one of the most proficient speakers of Two-Voice in the whole Compact; Desiree had always cautioned him about advertising that fact too loudly. He didn't need to put a target on his back for anyone who might try to climb over him to get to the top.

Two fellow Whispers in dark gray, crisp suits escorted him along the walkway leading up to the estate entrance. He recognized one—a petite brown woman with a deep, pink scar right below one of her eyes. She'd been one of the Whispers initially assigned to find his sister after she disappeared.

The mansion doors opened into a gigantic and opulent main hall. The ceiling seemed like it was in the clouds and Vade could hear the echo of every step he took. Stretched along one of the walls were three statues, each representing the source of the world's three magics; pain, pestilence and war.

"I didn't think you'd ever visit me again." Desiree called from the top of the staircase. An incredibly large portrait of the Compact's leader, President Koo, hung on the wall behind her. Koo's mischievous grin made it seem like he knew a secret and his long, white tresses made a narrow face look even longer. His brown skin was more than a few shades lighter than Vade's. Three silver chokers encircled his neck. Vade respected the man because of his position, not necessarily his fashion choices.

She descended the black staircase with all the regality and poise he expected her to, undiminished by the years. Desiree was a slender woman with pale skin and blonde hair reaching to her shoulders, a sharp nose and a soft chin. Age barely laid claim to her. Their paths would likely have never crossed if the Hyena Revenants hadn't bombed the chemical plant his parents worked at in Obuss, capital of the Amos-Morbine Compact. The explosion left him and Cyn orphans, until Desiree took them in. Gave them a purpose and made them Whispers. Their first mission had been to track down and eliminate every rebel in the Hyena Revenants. In that one operation they had the chance to fully avenge their parents and also learn in intricate detail how rebel networks were maintained. In a single decision, she had made them great, and healed Vade's heart.

He still swelled with gratitude at the sight of her.

"I would have visited sooner, but you keep me busy." Vade exchanged a bright smile with her.

Desiree laughed and they hugged at the bottom of the stairs. She was shorter than him now, but she'd never stopped feeling larger than life. The Amos-Morbine Compact owed more to her vision than any of those bureaucrats could ever realize. Vade thought they should just let her run the whole damn thing.

She stepped back and patted his chest. "You've been doing splendidly. So much progress in the field has happened because of your decisive actions."

Vade didn't think he could smile any harder. "It's for the empire. For the vision and a better world."

Her praise made Vade's shoulders light despite all
his recent doubts. Whatever he felt for Althus might be
a bump in the road, but it wasn't enough to bring his
journey to a halt. "Indeed. A world we can be proud
of." She turned and waved for him to follow. "Dinner
is just now being prepared. Catch me up on the Corrin
Islands."

He did as commanded, keeping the raunchier details out
of the briefing. Though she expected thorough reports, the
last thing he needed to do was dwell on Althus.

The dining room was another spectacle of polished
wood, expensive paintings and sparking silverware. The
dinner table could seat three dozen. He doubted Desiree
ever had more than ten people in this place, but she'd
taught him that prestige was found in aesthetics as often
as power. You needed to be able to show people what your
influence could offer them.

He spotted a bracelet next to one of the plates. He
recognized the lavender steel and the tiny golden skull
trinket from Obuss, the Compact's capital and Vade's
childhood home. Vade smiled at the sudden memory.
"From Cyn?"

Desiree looked back and smiled brighter. "I like to keep
reminders of my greatest students around. She was so
proud when she gave me that."

The jewelry had belonged to a rebel leader responsible
for poisoning the water supply of Edo Hill, a suburb of
Obuss. Dozens of people died and hundreds more were
left with incurable disease. There was outrage, but no one
had been more outraged than Cyn, especially seeing as
how the attacker had been from their hometown.

*"Those fuckers don't care who they hurt! Just like our parents."*

Cyn had tracked the woman down and killed her.
For a moment, remembering it almost made him feel
like his sister was in the room with them. But only for a
moment.

He sat across from Desiree at the end of the table while the house staff served them a meal of slow cooked pork shoulder, beans and cilantro rice. A simple meal so gorgeously presented; Vade whistled. "And here I was beginning to get used to hotel food."

Desiree smiled, but Vade noticed a tightness that hadn't been there before. "My Whispers deserve a good meal when they come to see me."

"As long as there's dessert!"

Desiree laughed. "Of course! There are a few cakes I've had the staff whip up. You can taste them all."

Growing up, she had been strictly against an overconsumption of sugar. She only relented to soften the delivery of hard truths. "What's going on, Desiree? You trained me too well to try and hide it."

"Indeed I have. It's about Cyn."

Vade stiffened.

She nodded over his shoulder. The petite Whisper who'd escorted him in approached and handed Desiree a metallic data core before taking a position at her shoulder. The Two-Voice-fueled devices allowed the Amos Morbine Compact to store and encrypt data that their imperial rivals couldn't decipher. Desiree accessed its contents briefly and laid it down on the table beside her plate. "Based on Yemaia's intel, we have now confirmed that the Phantom Dragons played a role in your sister's disappearance...and death."

Now he understood why Desiree refused to look at him. Even Yemaia kept her eyes down; his current assignment wasn't the best-kept secret.

Vade felt like he was tumbling down a black pit. "I thought—you said they weren't involved."

They'd been running through a long list of suspects for years. The Phantom Dragons were among the first they'd concluded had played no part in Cyn's disappearance.

"I was wrong."

"How could—"

"I wish I could claim perfection, but we both know that isn't true. I was wrong."

He held out a hand. "Let me take a look."

"You're too close to this Vade. I expect my Whispers to be thorough. You know that." Desiree looked miserable. "I never gave up on figuring out Cyn's disappearance and the details aren't spared in these files."

Information was key to discovery, she always said. How a target viewed details, especially the ones they left out, provided an intel treasure trove. "What did they do?"

"They sold her to the Exalted Fist sect based out of Enoch. Pale imitations of the originals that Yemaia and her team were able to wipe out." Desiree shook her head, giving a glance to the file. "She's dead now, Vade, but I'm so sorry. I would never have put you on such a slow burner operation if I thought for a second they had something to do with Cyn."

Vade wanted to scream. He wanted to break this table in half. He wanted to drag Althus back to the Corrin Islands and hold him under that pristine ocean until he drowned. Desiree was kind enough to not say it, but he knew a death like that wasn't a good one. Those anti-magic gangs were notorious for the cruelties they did to Whispers they captured. If he could, he'd bring them all right into the torture dimension and let its demons have their way with them.

His every thought was rage.

But unleashing that rage wasn't what Whispers did. He swallowed it, nearly gagging on the jagged edges. "What's next?"

"The Phantom Dragons are planning to attack me directly. I don't know or when," Desiree said. "You're a man of conviction. It's what I admire about you, and you've never killed when it wasn't necessary."

"What's next?" he asked again.

"The Phantom Dragons need to be ended. All of them."

There it was. Vade hated himself for not immediately thinking it would be the easiest thing in the world to do. But Althus had chosen his path.

"I could assign someone else to—"

"The fuck you will." Desiree frowned at him and Vade winced. She had demoted other people for less. "Sorry. I'm sorry. But it's Cyn."

"Understood." Desiree motioned to his plate. "Finish eating. You're not killing any rebels tonight."

But Vade's mind was already whirring through details. "Where are the others?"

"If you're on board, we'll arrange for you to enter Dyamaii. Yemaia's report indicates that Taigon and Akjo are operating in the Vo Forest towards some sort of political sabotage effort. Eliminate them and after that we can discuss how you'll tackle the rest."

"Absolutely. Cyn would expect no less."

Another Whisper came into the dining room and rushed to Desiree's side. "General Jonasu is calling and asked for you directly. Confirmed the proper communication codes."

General Jonasu was Desiree's equivalent of a sort in the Phobeta Courts. *Of a sort* because Vade doubted anyone was comparable to his mentor. Communication between them wouldn't be unheard of. It was part of the illusion of stable cooperation the three empires put on for the rest of the world. And the rebel groups were truly beginning to become a problem they needed to face together.

Desiree stood up. "I will be back, Vade. Please eat. The cooks are quite proud about today's dish. We wouldn't want to offend."

Vade shoved cilantro lime rice into his mouth, unable to taste any of it. He always knew things with Althus would have to end. But he never thought it would be like this.

# OLDERIANE

ALTHUS TOOK THE final step off his small, private plane onto the tarmac and drew in a deep breath. Olderiané still had a deep, earthy fragrance exactly like he remembered. Despite its urban sprawl, the city lacked the air pollution of other metropolises. Olderiane's locals resisted the empires' usual architecture and instead focused on infusing the natural with the urbane.

He'd chartered the plane using one of the Phantom Dragons' many shadow accounts. The paper trail behind them led to dozens of different false identities, usually situated right in the banking systems of the empires themselves. The airport in Olderiané was a dire thing in desperate need of repairs, but Althus knew that was on purpose. The locals hated imperial tourists and hoped a less than pristine arrival might make them unlikely to come back.

Althus took the Olderiané tactics to heart. They reminded him of one of Karmola's favorite phrases, often deployed when a Phantom Dragon wanted to rush off and do something stupid: *Not every fight requires a fist.*

The city's humidity was blistering. Waiting for him outside the airport was a small, blue car with a triangular hood: an old Amos-Morbine Compact model, once in fashion and now relegated to all the nations too poor to build their own automobiles. Yet another way that the world's beautiful places found themselves, whether by design or not, shores for the refuse of empire to wash upon. He sat in the backseat, thankful for the A/C, and gave the barest of glances to the driver, a muscular brown woman with rippling arms and harsh gray eyes. Althus knew she wouldn't say a word to him. The less she knew, the safer she'd be.

It had been two months since the vote was cast. He wasn't even sure that Vade would agree to meet him so soon after their last "vacation"—the spread between them was usually longer. But the Whisper had been all too eager to agree. Althus was suspicious, but he knew if he said so it would be seen as making excuses by the others, especially Karmola. And maybe it really was just an excuse. They were playing at being lovers. Who wouldn't be happy to see their boyfriend?

They rode across a long ass bridge to get out of the airport and into the heart of downtown. The streets were narrow, chaotic, and best navigated by a local. For every car, there were at least two solar-powered motorcycles and five elderly men on bikes in dire need of paint jobs. Horns honked and vibrant music played.

Althus could feel a goofy grin rising but he let it come. This was nice. This was distracting.

It was almost like he was actually here to enjoy the Festival of Bone Tails and not kill his lover. A Whisper. A dangerous, deadly killer. One that served at the behest of sycophants. Althus couldn't help but sink into the reality of that, to stew in his anger. He wanted the truth to drown out his doubts.

The truth had to be where he'd find the strength to do what was needed.

Though he supposed his plans brought him closer to the original notions behind the festival. Olderiané loved to tell stories of the beasts that once filled the world, whether they were the; golden-scaled manticores that flew over Obuss or the gigantic cobras with a hundred feathered wings that once hailed from the Courts. All those beasts were hunted down phantom dragons. Translucent and deadly, the otherworldly monsters showed no mercy. The Festival of Bone Tails was named after the gigantic remains that still litter the world as evidence of that ancient massacre.

Karmola inspiration from those stories when she formed the Phantom Dragons. Althus was now being asked to live up to the name. And he intended to.

The car finally slowed as it entered a part of downtown occupied by citizens unable to find shelter. Many were refugees from other nations wounded by conflict. Children walked among them. Just *one* of the rich fucks Vade served could fix this neighborhood in weeks.

Althus closed the door behind him as gently as possible, grabbed his suitcase out of the trunk, and let her go on her way. The city heat felt like the sticky hands of a child that wanted nothing less than to touch your face. At least he'd made sure to wear a white tank. Most clothes here leaned towards lighter colors in the day to bat away the sun. He moved away from the car quickly, the possibility of being tailed heavy on his mind. He'd need to be more vigilant than ever soon: the Amos-Morbine Compact would not easily forgive the killing of a Whisper.

That meant leaving as little a trail as possible—wanton destruction in the middle of a city would only be a beacon for the Amos-Morbine Compact to follow. He'd only seen the smallest use of it, but Vade was a master of Two-Voice. Althus had come to his own Two-Voice by illegal means—taught by a Compact deserter and practiced with Karmola—and wouldn't have half the brutal control a Whisper had over the torture dimension's language. As much as he was itching for a fight, Althus hadn't survived this long by being stupid. He couldn't beat a Whisper one-on-one. The only thing about dealing with Whispers every rebel group agreed on was that their fight meant your flight.

Down an alley, Althus spotted people dancing, while others were beating on trash cans to keep a rhythm going. If there was one thing Althus knew, joy was resistance too. Their energy was contagious—Althus nearly stopped and joined the party—but he didn't want to dilute their happiness with the intensity of his purpose.

He stopped at a door with a wooden viper nailed above it. The viper had been painted gold and had two luxurious black wings; there was a time when many great beasts walked the world, but now they were all gone and trinkets like this were some of the only things left to honor them. Even without the snake, Althus knew he was at the right place. The pristine condition of the welcome mat gave it away. The agent who lived here treated dust like it was a disease to be eradicated. Sajime always said that if she couldn't live a life of luxury, then she would at least make sure it was a clean one.

A chill up the back of his neck let him know he was being watched. Turning, he spotted a pair of eyes disappearing behind curtains of questionable quality. Althus frowned. This was a poorer neighborhood and the exploited had plenty of reason to be leery of outsiders, but something about it felt off. Maybe it was the whiplash of having just seen such joy. He shrugged it off.

Althus knocked.

Sajime opened the door with a boyish grin and leaned in way too close to Althus's face like a sibling itching for the chance to pester you. "Well hello hello! Figures you'd show up here. Always looking for the best places to have an orgasm."

Althus had a reputation and his fellows never missed a chance to jab at him about it. But who could blame him? Pretty men were to be enjoyed in pretty places. It wasn't his fault he had discerning taste. "I get it, you lost the vote. But don't take the shit out on me. You going to let me in before I freak out any more of your neighbors?"

"What do you mean?" Sajime fiddled with her crystal monocle and stepped out of the doorway.

"Someone across the street was spying on me and got spooked the minute I looked their way."

She considered the building behind him and then waved a dismissive hand. "There's a lot of people here doing things that we might call illegal. Doing what they need to survive. A pretty face like yours is bound to make them uneasy."

Her black nails glistened in the sun, almost distracting Althus from the tiny, lime green sores spread thinly across them. Althus rolled his eyes and headed inside. Like his stolen Two-Voice, Sajime was an illegal Blacknail. Her magic came from the cancer dimension controlled by the Enoch Consortius. The sores were one of the costs she paid for wielding her magic. Althus knew the day would come when he'd have to pay his own price too—speaking Two-Voice would one day rob him of his ability to say anything at all.

As soon as he brought in his suitcase, Althus was overwhelmed by the scent of lavender. Dozens of candles burned on tables and windowsills. He tried not to cough. "I don't know how you've managed to remain unnoticed as long as you have if the whole district can smell your spot."

"I don't stay in the same house for more than a few weeks, you know that." She motioned with long, powerful arms to encompass the entirety of her abode.

"Can you at least blow a few out if I'm going to be staying here?"

"No, because you are by no means staying. You're here to arrange your exit strategies and that's it." She rubbed a sweaty shirt against the monocle. "Karmola's whole fucking plan is deranged. She's going to make us the Compact's primary target and then we're all dead."

"It's one Whisper, Sajime."

"Yea and just a few protests landed my ass in a prison. Trust me, Althus, empires already get off on torturing people like us. If we go and kill one of their prized possessions…"

Althus clenched his jaw. "I don't do sloppy. They'll never know it was us."

"Even you don't believe that, Althus."

"Don't doubt me. Remember who fixed your revolution in Tinhadinys?"

"Please. I had that situation under control. But—it was nice having you help me get all that slime out of my hair." She gave a false shiver, ran a hand through her slick ponytail and smiled, but it quickly fizzled out when she realized Althus wasn't returning the expression. Sajime sighed. "I'm sorry. Things have just been tense here. The added heat Karmola's plan will stir up isn't going to help."

"Don't hold back. Might as well lay it on me." Althus didn't personally subscribe to random bursts of venting, but it helped some people. And despite all the snark, Sajime was a friend. A good one. They'd been in some tough spots together.

"It's the Phobeta Courts. They've been picking off a lot of my informants."

"Fucking Paleskins. Think there's a snitch in the works?" The Phantom Dragons cultivated allies in many different rebel groups, the quiet resistors in the imperial governments, and generally people who were tired of the way the world had failed them all. What they called the works was the product of years and the small changes people made along

the way. Vade was certainly a different man than when he
started. But the works was by no means perfect. A snitch
wasn't unheard of.

"No. We're just getting sloppy, making mistakes."
Sajime made a valiant attempt at beating back the heat
with a fan. "Karmola and her obsession with the Onyx
Cabin is going to get us all killed."

"The intel suggests she's right, though. If even a quarter
of what's supposed to be in there actually is, we would
have enough global intelligence to facilitate hundreds of
meaningful operations."

Sajime motioned for Althus to follow her. She led
him through a narrow hallway flanked with paintings
of women warriors battling monsters. The paintings
were autographed with the lilting, blooming consonants
of Mabbic, the language spoken in most of the Enoch
Consortius. They passed a small statue of a headless
manticore to enter a dimly lit basement dominated by a
long metal table stacked with gray boxes full of papers.
Sajime manufactured most forged documentation within
the Phantom Dragon's operations. If you needed to sneak
by some stuffy, underpaid government official, Sajime
was the person you came to. Running forgeries for other
groups also gave the Phantom Dragons a nice revenue
stream to keep up their own activities.

"You need to be careful," Sajime said, stacking up all
the necessary documents Althus would need to make a
smooth getaway from Olderiané. "This is a Whisper. He'll
fuck you a lot harder than usual if you aren't careful."

"I was a soldier, Sajime." The most pitiful kind, but one
nonetheless.

"I know you're good at what you do, but again, he's a
Whisper."

"Look, if he takes me down then you and Karmola can
tag team his ass."

"I'm also not fighting a damn Whisper. My ass is running."

As Sajime handed over the falsified documents, the intense odor of onions and rot permeated the room. Sajime's eyes widened and Althus silently cursed. They both knew they had only a few moments before Paleskins would be on them.

"Neighbors, huh?" Althus raised an eyebrow.

"You're the one they saw!"

Althus shut his eyes tight. "You are *not* putting this on me."

"I'm not." Sajime's nails grew and sparked. "Just fuck you for being right."

As if the smell weren't enough, Paleskins moved as if both gravity and reality didn't apply to them. Three of them, Executioner rank, slid through the basement wall like a hand moving through water, the teeth in their stupid grins white enough to almost disappear against their ashen skin. They wore black bodysuits with exposed fingers and sharp shoulder pads emblazoned with the Phobeta Court's emblem, a viper holding a ball of fire in its mouth.

"Sajime Kass, you are hereby ordered executed by decree of the Phobeta Courts!"

They wouldn't waste time reasoning with Paleskins; if they hit first, you'd already lost. Space operated differently for them. Letting them close with you gave them a ridiculous advantage.They would reach right into your chest and pull out your heart like a spoon scooping ice cream. Althus called on Two-Voice. "*Ronari pevalu.*"

After everyone heard him say "Burn the sandwich," one of the Paleskin's eyes went wide—at least one of them had some situational awareness."Two-Voice! Go for him!"

But Althus's spell was already in play; hours spent training with Akjo meant that Althus could pick apart a Paleskin in a way no regular Two-Voicer could. Glowing purple bands clamped around their necks until the Phobeta Court killers gagged in mid-air, clawing at them, trying desperately to slide through the bands just like they did everything else.

The Paleskins tried to sink into the ground, but they only managed to get as far as their necks until they rose back out of the wood screaming. "Damn it, they could try and give these bastards perfume or something."

"It's going to take days to get this smell out." Sajime pressed a finger against the Paleskin's foreheads. Each time, her eyes rolled back as a spark of blue light spread from her fingertips and across them. She stepped back as their bodies convulsed and Althus's magic faded away.

The Paleskins wanted to scream but their own tongues had grown too large for their mouths. Unnatural green veins spread along their faces until the veins burst open and hundreds of small white vines poured out of them. Like starving beasts, the vines consumed all, crunching bones and dissolving flesh until they were satiated, became brittle and faded to ash.

"Assholes," Althus muttered.

Sajime uttered a string of colorful curses as she grabbed a roll of trash bags from a cabinet. "I've kept this place off their trail for *years*. Fuckers!"

Althus grabbed some towels from upstairs to help clean up the viscera. "These aren't your good ones right?"

Sajime frowned. "They're *all* my good ones, Althus."

"Clean freak. Got it." He picked up a scrap of meat that might have been a liver. "Lighting some candles down here might be a good move."

Sajime gagged as she filled a trash bag. "Don't start with me."

"So what now? You going to get out of Olderiane?"

Sajime looked torn. "I don't know. This is my city. And even if I did, I don't think I should go until you take care of that Whisper."

Althus squirmed at the camaraderie. "You don't have to stay for me."

"Oh, cut the stoic fuckboi routine. I think Karmola's plan is fucking shit, but Phantom Dragons don't abandon each other. Besides, the vote was cast. You're the guy for the job and Karmola would whine if I didn't help you."

"Karmola whine? We must be talking about a different person."

"You've been around that scumbag Whisper too long. She's changed, Althus."

*That Whisper.* It rankled. That was what he *should* be referring to Vade as. Maybe it was all subterfuge, but the man made him feel good, even if he hated himself for it.

"Either way, we came to a consensus."

The cleaning done, Sajime began packing with all the nervous energy that came after just killing someone. "Right. Get to your location and I'll get to mines. We'll find each other once the bastard's finished."

# DYAMAII — THE VO FOREST

**V**ADE KEPT TO the shadows, crouching close against the thick trees of the forest, ensuring he was not followed. The chill ocean breeze whistled around him and through the branches. It made for a strange music the locals called ignai, the blessing of nature, portents of good fortune. The sound allowed him to hope he'd find out something concrete about Cyn's fate.

The brown granite building he arrived at looked like it could comfortably house three people. Foliage had started to invade and conquer its flat roof and a few chem-lights were on, burning a harsh yellow. He took a breath and steadied his heart rate. He'd planned this strike after observing the building for days. The Phantom Dragons would be meeting with local informants tonight. He had done operations like this dozens of times.

Tension bunched up his shoulders as he stalked towards the safe house. This was it. No turning back.

*"Acon cex lenu ras temma,"* he said quietly.

Two Phantom Dragons would be here tonight. Black flames rippled across Vade's arms and flared in his eyes. No heat emitted from them, but they warmed him with power all the same. He ran the remaining distance to the safehouse with a gazelle's swiftness. At the last possible moment, he leapt, balling his body up and crashing through a window. Shouts erupted as his feet touched the ground.

Three of five seated at the table inside panicked, scrambling for an exit and tripping over themselves in the process. The other two, as expected, were the Phantom Dragons Akjo and Taigan. Vade wasn't foolish enough to think they weren't dangerous, but he also wasn't about to let either one get in the way of him finding answers.

"Hope I'm not interrupting anything important," Vade drawled.

Akjo's face spasmed with fury. Not exactly a face becoming of a former priest. He had turned his back on the Crimson Pages when they started receiving hefty financial backing from the Phobeta Courts. Ironic, considering the man now employed the magic of the Phobeta Courts as a Paleskin. Vade wondered how he disguised the typical scent associated with that magic. He doubted he'd just be able to ask. The black wraps around his hands and forearms were sure marks of a fighter, not a talker, and his bare feet had calluses that could break bricks.

Akjo came at him fast with uncanny reaction time. Vade dodged and flung a knife at Taigan, pinning his hand to the wall. Akjo fell into the ground like a bullet and surfaced behind Vade just as quickly. He barely dodged Akjo's punch and grabbed his attacker's wrist before he could become intangible again and flung him into the table. There was a satisfying cacophony of broken wood and spilled cutlery.

Fighting a Paleskin was all about timing. You had to attack in the moments right when they tried to strike you.

Otherwise, you'd spend your whole time on the defensive. Vade leapt across the space separating them with a high kick, but Taigon snatched his ankle and sent Vade crashing into a glass vase.

Angry steam practically blew out Taigon's large nostrils and past his charcoal-colored septum ring as he flashed teeth sharpened to points. The display made Vade clumsy for just a moment; they marked Taigon as a member of the Exalted Fist, a rebel group that Vade and Cyn had hunted down. Vade hadn't know there were any survivors. How had he missed that?

"Imperial scumbag!" Taigon swung at him with a right hook.

Vade got underneath it but wasn't fast enough—Taigon's knee connected with the left side of his face. He went rolling to the side and Akjo came up through the ground again, successfully landing an uppercut. Vade did his best to protect his face, but that left his ribs open to Taigon. The two Phantom Dragons were wailing on him. He'd black out soon if he didn't do something.

*How dare they touch what's mine! Let me in. Let me crush them.* The voice made him twitch; a fight came down to seconds. He'd never imagined giving in to it, but the choices you made in a small space of time determined victory or defeat.

He gave in to the voice.

Vade couldn't describe the feeling. Ecstasy laced with a terrible burning, like getting your hand cut off right when you were cumming and feeling a deep, sick compulsion to want more. *There is so much more. Let me show you.* His mouth tasted like copper, but he had what he needed.

Power.

The tide of the battle changed so fast that neither of the Phantom Dragons were aware of the shift. Vade spat blood on the floor and the words needed to end this —words he's never spoken before—fell rapid fire from his mouth. "*Drinay aigo nlak ifud'e.*" The Phantom Dragons were lifted off their feet. Vade had complete control over them. He held power over every plant in the forest, every bug on the leaves, every bird in the air. And it felt right. As it should be.

The flesh of Akjo and Taigan was like clay in his hands. He didn't look at them as he squeezed, but he couldn't ignore their pain or the way their bodies contorted as they died. The lifeforce he took from the Dragons and everything around him tasted sweet on his tongue. It left him more revitalized than he'd felt in years. If he held onto what the voice's spell gave him, he might be able to fight an army and yet—

*Don't push me away.* But he did. He pushed the demon away. Because what else could the voice have been all this time but a demon?

The rush of power retreated and Vade collapsed to his knees, surrounded by the violent results of his confrontation. Viscera covered the walls like a fresh coat of paint. A desiccated finger lay not far away from Taigon's septum rings. He hadn't seen a massacre this violent since the day they thought they'd destroyed the Exulted Fists. Cyn had wiped away Vade's vomit when the fight was over and the adrenaline left him.

But Cyn wasn't here to help this time.

A new horror awaited him when he clawed his way back into the thick, night air. The Dyamaii forest was… gone. The moon's light left nothing unseen: the leaves had turned brown, trees turned to a sloppy gray sludge, and the animals skeletal. The demon's power had done this— Vade had done this. Vade fell to his knees. How could he?

*I have so many gifts for you.*

No, he told himself. He never wanted to feel this way ever again. But his body already ached for more.

# OLDERIANE — MAGIC LOUNGE

AFTER SPENDING hours staking out the Cane Towers from a Magic Lounge room across the street, Althus knew something was wrong as soon as Vade got out of the car. His dress shirt was wrinkled, he had grease stains on his pants, and the bags under his eyes were darker than he'd had ever seen them. The sexiest thing about Vade was usually his unshakeable cool. None of that was present now. Whatever happened before his arrival had messed him up bad.

Althus still couldn't help but want to lay his head on Vade's shoulder. What kind of fool was he? If he kept this up, he'd walk himself into a freshly dug grave.

"He's damn pretty," Sajime said with a chuckle after she took the binoculars. "You're lucky you got to bone him as long as you did."

Althus didn't have it in him to join in on the teasing. He'd crumble. "Vade's a Whisper. We both know what kind of bastards they are and the trail of bodies they leave."

"Yeah, they're real pieces of shit," Sajime agreed. "I have a confession."

"Am I sure I want to know?"

"It'll help a few things make sense." Sajime wiped a line of sweat from her forehead. "One of my contacts figured out that the Amos-Morbine Compact has been doing new experiments with the torture dimension. They're trying to draw on another kind of magic from there. Something bigger than Two-Voice. But I wasn't the first Phantom Dragon my contact sold the intel to."

Althus connected the dots. "Karmola. Is that why she was so dead set on us moving so fast? But what if they talked to someone *sympathetic* to the Compact?"

Sajime shrugged. "I doubt it. These people survive on knowing who *not* to talk to. But my contact was definitely feeding shit to the Phobeta Courts. It's why they're on my ass."

Althus scowled and took his binoculars back to watch the valet taking Vade's luggage. If the Amos-Morbine Compact had found a new terrible way to use the magic of the torture dimension, it could tip the scales of power entirely in their favor. The Enoch Consortius and the Phobeta Courts would either have to up the ante, find something in their respective dimensions, or it wouldn't just be war. It'd be a slaughter. The ramifications brought Althus back into focus. "Fuck. Karmola's scared."

"And impulsive. I don't think the Compact knows we're involved. My contact hated working for them. Screwing the Compact over was their mission in life."

"I hope so. The Compact really does want us all dead or under their thumb, huh?"

"An endless pursuit of power guarantees endless violence," Sajime agreed.

"Huh." Althus noticed the silver necklace Vade wore. Althus had given it to him last year as a birthday gift.

He'd known it wasn't Vade's real birthday, but Althus had treated it with all the thought a real one entailed. Looking back, it had been one of many ill-advised steps leading him to his current situation.

"You alright, Althus?"

"Yeah. Fine." He did his best to look merciless. To look like this mission would be like any other. "Just make sure my escape routes are good to go. Once I get this bastard, I'm going to have to run fast."

# OLDERIANE — ANIDA'S MARVELS

**O**LDERIANE WAS WORLD famous for its candy shops and Vade's favorite of them was Anida's Marvels. Their candied insects were without peer. He remembered the first time he swallowed one of Anida's sour beetle wings—he hadn't realized they were supposed to be chewed and nearly ended up choking.

Dyamaii weighed on Vade but he had to keep his cover intact: a well-to-do businessman who sought luxury in all his travels. Keeping up this act was a matter of survival—the Whispers couldn't take official responsibility for Dyamii. No one in his government could be allowed to know what havoc he had brought down. He dreaded Desiree finding out the details. Being a weapon for the Amos-Morbine Compact was a delicate thing. Whispers had to be efficient enough to scare those around him, but not so powerful they felt safer with him dead.

Vade had made sure to plant evidence that would implicate the Cotati Legion in what happened at Vo Forest.

Provoking in-fighting amongst rebel groups was a tried-and-true tactic. Few of the groups agreed on much and leveraging that discord was an easy out. But a gnawing part of him felt guilty. For now, he needed to do his job. So Vade walked the streets alone in this upscale neighborhood and took in the sights.

"Hello! Back so soon eh?" Anida, the shop owner, stood behind her counter.

"You remember me?"

"Can't forget the handsome ones." Anida smiled, her teeth yellowed with age, but much more intact than one might expect from a candy shop owner.

Vade returned the smile. "Mind if I browse around a bit?"

"Of course not." She winked at him. "You're one of my favorite customers."

He stood in front of the pronged blue raspberries. The berries were dipped in a vat of boiled sugar and left to harden. To appeal to foreigners, the candies were each inscribed with a different character from Kohi, the language of the Phobeta Courts. A wrong stroke gave a character an entirely different meaning and Vade had noticed plenty of errors over the years. Still, he could go through three jars of these in a day and not blink. Given how stressed he was now, he might need about six. But as he reached up to grab one of the jars, something in his reflection in the glass reminded him of Akjo and Taigan's twisted, broken faces. Vade yanked his hand back and nearly crashed into the shelves behind him.

Anida was there right quick. "Are you alright?"

"I'm sorry." Vade gave a weak laugh and shook his head. "Thought I saw a bug and got startled."

The shop owner's smile returned. "No worries! The critters here are a bunch of little bastards."

When he was once again out of sight, Vade closed his eyes and rolled his head around until he could feel the tension fade.

But he couldn't shake that image. He should probably seek help, but he wasn't a fool. Whispers needed to always be in control. He'd be given no more chances to find out what happened to Cyn. His sister deserved better.

He paid for a few jars of the candy, and barely said goodbye to Anida before he stumbled out the door.

Dyamaii had changed him. He'd let it change him. The demon's power had been so…invigorating. Just like when he was with Althus. It disgusted him, but he couldn't stop thinking about it. He didn't realize he'd arrived back at the hotel until he saw Althus in the busy lobby. His lover stood beside the water fountain sculpted to look like the inside of a cave with a river slicing down its middle. Vade's breath caught. Althus wasn't supposed to be here. What if…

The seconds felt like hours.

Before he could question himself, Vade rushed across the lobby, took Althus's face in his hands, and kissed him. Deeply. This moment, this happiness, was enough to block out the whole world. *This* was the world he wanted to live in. A world where his work as a Whisper and Althus's misbegotten politics didn't matter. And the closer it all came to ending, the more Vade wanted to slow down and enjoy it while he could. If only it didn't make him feel so guilty.

When Vade had to accept that those years couldn't be found in this hotel lobby, Althus smiled up at him. "That was nice. Worked up already huh? It hasn't been that long."

"It's been long enough." Vade knew how stupid it was to let his guard down here, but he grabbed Althus's belt buckle and pulled him closer. "Let's go upstairs."

"We have plenty of time later." Althus put his hand on top of Vade's. He held a black card embossed with silver writing "I reserved a table for us later. Show the bouncer when you get there."

"Just the two of us?" Vade took the card. "No local friends you want to invite?"

"I have friends everywhere." Althus pressed a finger against Vade's chest. "It's you I want to be with."

He didn't know yet, Vade decided, and summoned a smirk. "Can't argue with that."

"Good. I'll see you tonight then." Althus kissed him on the cheek and left.

Vade's chest pounded harder with each step Althus took from him as the end of all this drew that much closer. Tonight. In a fairer world, Althus would have followed him to his room, and they would have made love before he could even open the door. Instead, he would find out what Althus knew, and if he wouldn't fall into line, he would do what Desiree and the Amos-Morbine Compact required of him.

He twisted the black card between his fingers.

Tonight.

# OLDERIANE

CANE TOWERS WERE on the touristy side of Olderiané:
full of overpriced restaurants, expensive hotels and
dressed up hostels trying to pass themselves off as
chic. Althus noticed a few street performers and grifters,
but they would be removed before nightfall along with
the rest of the local flare. The Festival of Bone Tails was a
thing to be experienced, and the imperial tourism board
had an expectation they'd be able to do it in one piece.

Althus circled the block a few times, popping into a
couple of different hotels for a quick drink to throw off
any tails. When he was sure he wasn't followed, he went
back to his room in the Magic Lounge, and flopped on
a bed of risky sturdiness. What was wrong with Vade?
His shoes were scuffed, his pants wrinkled, and there was
a cut on his neck Althus was sure he hadn't put there.
Something had rattled him so much that he couldn't even
keep his cover straight. Was he in danger? What could put
a Whisper in a situation where they came off that frantic?

Part of Althus wondered if maybe Vade had seen the error of his ways and wanted to leave the Compact behind. But as soon as that thought came, Althus smothered it. He had agreed to this task and trying to find ways out of it did not help the Phantom Dragons.

And what did Vade mean by *friends*? They were always alone when they saw each other. Sure, they both threw out a few random names to create the appearance of a larger life, but they never actually met anyone. For Vade to bring it up now could mean the man was trying to tell him something.

He hopped up from his bed. Being alone wasn't going to do him any favors right now. He rented a motorbike and headed to a neighborhood across town full of cafes and little eateries with irreverent names meant to mock empires, like Rancid Provisions and Black Graves Brewery. The smells coming from each of them were a pleasant assault on his nostrils. He grabbed a batch of rice from a stall—Amos Mambo Combo—before making his way to the little blue building where Sajime worked most days.

The red letters above the door were in the native language of Sajime's island home, Dyamaii. Althus couldn't pronounce them properly, but they meant *All wounds are welcome here*. Sajime took care of her patients free of charge.

Althus swallowed a mouthful as he entered and nodded at the medic at the desk, a fat man with intensely attractive lips. He wondered what battlefield this guy had walked away from—Sajime's employees practiced the kind of medicine most learned resisting the machinations of empire. "Just here to see Sajime."

The man wasn't immediately charmed by Althus. "You must be what has her in such a shitty mood. She's in the back."

"Uhh…thanks." He gave the medic a quick nod and headed towards her office.

Though the place had been once painted in a calming sky blue, it needed a touch-up. A few of the chem-lights buzzed on and off. It reminded Althus of the therapy clinics back in Tashedin—one-time simplicity dulled by years of disregard. But if he'd already annoyed Sajime, he wasn't going to start giving out any decorating tips.

Sajime called out to him before he even got to her door. "You're lucky I don't have any patients right now or I'd kick your ass out."

Althus poked his head in and summoned a mischievous grin. "Come on, you really can't hate me being here that much."

"It's the Festival of Bone Tails! I hate everyone from out of town right now. All my favorite places are packed with you annoying assholes." She glanced at his food. "Vicardo Rice! I love that shit."

"I thought it was—"

Sajime held up a finger to cut him off. "They changed the name to make more tourists buy it. Can't be *too* foreign for imperials."

"I see where the front desk guy gets the pissiness from."

"He doesn't like anyone." Sajime flipped through a stack of medical records from behind her desk. "Why are you here? Shouldn't you be getting ready?"

"I don't really want to be alone right now. Needed to clear my head."

"Our work isn't easy." She put the stack down and pulled out a bottle from a desk drawer. "Don't have any glasses."

Althus assessed the label. "Rochadi vintage?"

Her Luminous Natalis VI, leader of the Enoch Consortius, was painted on the bottle. She'd long ago mandated that her image be pictured on all her government's most prized exports. Her fruit serum-tinted red eyes were meant to be a sign of superiority and her bald brown head had been tattooed with white butterflies. Althus thought the black lipstick gave her a feral quality.

"Straight from the island where the Consortius ran things before selling our land to the Phobetans. Cost me a damn lot. Would have been more, but I got a few cousins who work at the port back home." Sajime handed the bottle to Althus. "Got another one on the way, so don't be shy."

The bottle was heavy as shit; a good swing could crack someone's head open. He did a couple of curls with it and got a laugh out of Sajime. Seeing her smile made him feel good. He unscrewed the bottle and took a long swig of the thick, yellow liquid inside. It was sweet and hot going down his throat.

"I shouldn't feel like shit, Sajime, but I do."

"If you didn't feel bad it would mean you're getting numb to all this." Sajime snatched the bottle back from Althus. She leaned back and took a swig; the chem-lights made her crystal monocle sparkle. "Did I ever tell you where Karmola found me?"

"A prison or something right?" Althus was fuzzy on the details and the liquor wasn't helping, but he knew Sajime was in a bad way when she was brought into the Phantom Dragons. He wasn't keen on having to share details about his own past, so he'd never asked.

"A Phobetan prison in the middle of the Red Ice Ocean. Run by Paleskins as an organ farm. It was nothing to them to dip into someone's body and take out a liver or a bone. Fucking monsters." Sajime had a distant look in her eye. "Karmola came in the dead of night on one damn boat. Can you believe that? But she tore the place apart. Took out the guards. Freed us all."

"So she took you in?"

"Not right away. At first, she just agreed to drop me off somewhere and let me find my own way. But I think my anger resonated with her. I couldn't go home—that would just bring the Courts down on my family. And she saw how much I wanted to tear it all down."

"She saved me too. You all did." And here he was, less sure of himself than ever.

"That anger would have gotten me killed without her."

Althus took another swig of the Rochadi instead of answering.

"Maybe we can do something to hold off on the kill order," Sajime offered. "See if there isn't another way to neutralize the threat he poses."

Althus wasn't going to ask for that. "My emotions don't matter here. I have work to do."

Something rattled inside Sajime's desk. She drew her eyebrows together and pulled out a small white box. A new letter had been sent through. She hummed, her nails glistenening, until the tiniest of blue vines inched out of her fingertips, covering the entire box, then hardening and crumbling to ash. Althus suspected that anyone who touched the box before Sajime unlocked it would have had something very unpleasant happen to them.

Sajime unfolded a note and started to read. Her humming stopped and tears came to her eyes. "Akjo and Taigan. They're dead."

Cold dread wormed its way up Althus's spine. "What? When?"

"A few days ago. The forest is...destroyed? How can that be?" Sajime rubbed the bridge of her nose. "One of the knives left behind points to the Cotati Legion, but that doesn't make any sense."

No. No, it didn't. Althus set down the bottle as understanding grew in him. This explained it. This explained all of it. The disheveled appearance. The scratch on his neck. The look of an animal ready to run away.

Vade had done this. Althus was almost grateful—now he had no more doubts. Vade had to die and he had to be the one to do it.

# OLDERIANE — THE DISCORDANT HEART

THE LONG, RAUCOUS line to the club wrapped around the corner, which Vade reckoned was manufactured to bring in more business. Most folks in town for the festival were looking to have some fun or to take someone back to their overpriced hotels once the party died down. Vade could pick out which country many of them were from by what they wore. The Phobetan women wore necklaces of black flowers, a nod to a current musical craze there. Most Phobetan men had five silver earrings on their right ear, as a marker of their refusal to be pressed into military service. A few of the Phobetans in the line wore both. Plenty of thigh high boots on folks from the Enoch Consortius and it seemed like many of the young men from the eastern Amos-Morbine Compact were styled in a new trend of corsets trimmed with spikes and temporary, but extravagant manticore tattoos on their necks.

Vade felt old. These were kids: fresh, vibrant, and still unbroken by the ugliness of the world. They were holding hands, sneaking kisses, singing to songs they hoped to hear later. Stupid and as impossible as it sounded, he wanted to have one more night of genuine, unmitigated fun with Althus. But it could never happen now. He had the blood of Phantom Dragons on his hands. There wasn't going to be any coming back from that.

*The Discordant Heart* beamed the blue letters above the club's door; the E in *heart* had been replaced with the symbol of the organ. He was getting too old for all this. He looked down at the black invitation and took a big breath. This was it. No turning back.

He walked past the line and straight up to the front where a bouncer stood with folded arms. Her jaw looked strong enough to chew through chains and she had a big scar across her right eye. Vade held up the black card between two fingers. "Got an invite."

She snatched it out of his hands and looked it over. She wasn't the least bit intimidated by him; his cover must be effective. She handed it back with a shrug. "Sorry. Got a lot of people who think they're Olderiané's biggest star and should be let in because they look nice."

Vade smiled. "Well, thank you for thinking I look nice."

The bouncer snickered. "Go inside already." She jabbed a thumb behind her. Murals of the blue heart from the club logo being pulled from a corpse were splashed across the black walls of the dimly lit dancehall, otherwise lit only by the chem-lights flashing between white, red, and blue as they illuminated sections of the club to the beat of the music. Olderiane's charts favored thumping rhythms full of hard cymbal crashes. Not Vade's favorite, but you could fall into it after an hour or so. The club wasn't packed yet, leaving the long bar's sleek black marble countertop mostly empty. The bartenders all had geometric sidecuts, ties, and long-chained nose rings that extended from their nostril to their ear.

At the far end of the bar, Althus nursed a drink. A sting of bittersweetness hit Vade in the chest. This would be the last time they played this game.

Normally, Vade would find someone else in the room and flirt for a bit, catching a few glances Althus's way. Create distance. Spark the first embers of desire. The fragility of that illusion now was painful; tonight would be so much easier if he had never let his walls down. Then he could see this mission as standard protocol and as—

He flagged down one of the bartenders, who smiled and cupped their ear to hear Vade's order. "Just an Azul and Crown please."

He set down enough money to pay for three of the drinks. It didn't take them long to bring it back to him in a tall, thin glass. "Threw an extra shot in there for you."

"You're the best."

He sipped the tart drink and sidled a little closer to Althus. He hadn't looked Vade's way the entire time. Every little movement that brought him closer gave Vade an ache at what was to come.

Althus wore a dark purple button-down that exposed most of his chest, complemented by thigh-hugging black pants and boots. He finally acknowledged Vade with a quick up and down glance.

Vade felt a jolt of hunger despite himself.

Althus bit his lip and stared at Vade's crotch just long enough to make a point. "You from here?"

"No. Just in town on business." Vade leaned an elbow on the bar and smirked. "But I could be persuaded to have some fun."

"Fun? I wouldn't know the concept."

Vade laughed. "I don't believe that for a second."

"So what do you believe?"

The question shouldn't have hit so hard but it did. What did Vade believe? He believed the two of them deserved a better world than the one that had been dealt to them.

"I believe a man like you shouldn't be alone." He was right on Althus then, lips nearly touching. "Ever."

"Who says I'm alone?" Althus teased, looking out to the dancefloor.

...*fuck!* Althus might not be alone. Vade should have done a better sweep of the place before saddling into his game. Vade refused to panic. "Then maybe whoever he is can just watch." Vade held Althus's lower back and turned him slowly, surveying the room. They were still only a breath away from each other.

"Right here?" Althus's question was full of want.

Vade reached for the other man's drink and took a slow sip. "Anywhere with you, sexy. Anywhere at all."

The game was over, and they kissed. Vade sat his drink down to cup Althus's face. He needed to capture the passion of this moment; there would be no more kisses like this after tonight.

"You still drinking that nasty ass cocktail?" Althus asked, turning his nose up at Vade's glass. The drink he held was much smaller and darker.

"Better than the gasoline you call alcohol."

Althus grinned. "Imported from the Consortius. Didn't think they'd have it."

"With all the tourists here, they'd be stupid not to."

"You know who's supposed to be playing here tonight?" Vade asked, trying to get back into the present.

Althus produced a small, clear bag. "It won't really matter once we take one of these."

The things inside looked like small crimson gummies. Necro-worms. Addicts became immortal wraiths with sunken eyes and fading gray skin, forever craving their next high. But they'd done them together a few times before and Vade would be lying if he said he didn't enjoy them. They gave him a body high, euphoria, and even a ridiculous sex drive. Doing drugs on assignment wasn't a good idea, but neither was breaking cover, so he had a choice to make.

"I'll take two to start," Vade said, holding out his hand as Althus dropped them in his palm. He only threw one of the worms down his throat, a compromise, not taking the time to chew. Make his stomach work a little harder.

The necro-worms seeped through his system in a tide of calm. For some, this mental peak created a slight moment of panic, but he had only ever known peace from it. Right before all of its glorious charm worked its way through his mind.

He took Althus's hand. "Let's dance."

For a while, they were immortal. It was only them and the music. The chem-lights bathed them in flashing colors. The anxious bass lines and heavy vocals added a darkness to their bodies' rhythm. Vade felt powerful. They were above it all.

They bounced to the music in that young, horny crowd, bodies pressed against each other. Althus's face buried in his neck as Vade gripped the other man's hips, his ass. He nibbled Althus's ear and received the softest moan in response. The demon moaned too and pleasure shivered from Vade's torso to his groin. Vade trembled even more when Althus snuck a finger into his waistband and teased him, right there on the dancefloor.

Minutes turned to hours. Althus left to get them bottles of water, but they were downed quickly in favor of more kisses. Like a bee to pollen, Vade did as nature intended and brought Althus back into his arms. Their sweat was cold, a small side effect of this kind of pleasure. Vade enjoyed its chill against his fingertips as he ran his hand down Althus's open chest. When they kissed, it was like time stopped but their bodies kept moving. Eternity was theirs on the dance floor and Vade refused to give it up.

Vade couldn't remember wanting anything but this. "I missed you." He crushed Althus against him, trying to pull him even closer.

"Me too," Althus said in Vade's ear, making him quiver and keeping him rock hard. "Let's go to our room. It should be ready."

They got through the crowd with a mix of apologies and smiles as they bumped into people, sometimes stopping to dance with strangers amidst a building sense of anticipation. They followed signs past a dozen thick frosted glass doors. Blacknail enchantments, calcified fungal symbols, were emblazoned on each of them. Vade assumed that was how they kept people from sneaking into the rooms. Expensive shit and a gratuitous waste of power.

"We're here." Althus pressed his black card against the symbols on the last door. The glass hissed and emitted a soft scent of vanilla. Althus looked back at him with a hungry smile, but something was off. What was it?

"This place is huge." Althus dropped onto one of the plush neon couches. He kicked a leg over the armrest and slowly unbuttoned the remainder of his shirt.

"Plenty of room for us to dance." Vade wasn't as delicate. Maybe he was naive, but if this illusion was about to shatter he wanted to revel in it first. He peeled his shirt off and laid his body on the couch, pressing against Althus chest to chest.

Vade's lips hovered just away from Althus's for a moment as his hand wandered down Althus's stomach. He took him in with a long, passionate kiss. Althus bit and held Vade's lip as he pulled away—it made Vade rock hard. He began a trail of hungry kisses from Althus's collarbone to his belt.

Vade gripped the buckle in his teeth and pulled until it popped off.

*Yes. Take him. Consume him.*

Vade took what he needed out of Althus's pants and buried it all in one swallow.

Althus arched back and let out a long sigh, but this had become about Vade's pleasure. Between the demon and the drugs, he worked on Althus with unquenchable lust, wrist spasming as he stroked himself. This was his last chance to enjoy Althus. He was going to put every passion and regret he had into getting them both to finish.

# OLDERIANE — THE DISCORDANT HEART

ALTHUS' STOMACH SANK at the desperation in Vade's kiss. But it served its purpose, getting him into this vulnerable position. It was time to reveal himself.

"*Frino eedu zek.*" Two-Voice flowed out of Althus in a whisper.

Vade's body stiffened and his eyes widened. If he hadn't known Two-Voice himself, he would have heard, "There's no more time."

Spittle frothed at the corner of Vade's mouth as he struggled to talk.

Althus had betted on the numbing effects of the necro-worms to slow down Vade's reflexes. It had paid off. Instead of taking one himself, he'd eaten a gummy worm from Anida's Marvels.

The music was still thumping, the party nowhere close to stopping, and the head bouncer (a friend of the Phantom Dragons) had ensured him no staff would be nearby. He'd be able to end a violent operative's life, use Two-Voice to make sure no one remembered seeing him come in here, slip out, and be long gone before the Discordant Heart realized they had a dead Whisper on their hands.

And yet tears rolled down, his cheeks. "Why couldn't you be different? I thought—" Althus said, his voice cracking.

Althus drew his blade, a crescent-shaped black instrument. It had been given to him by Karmola when she welcomed him into the Phantom Dragons. Using it now felt like a re-declaration of loyalty.

He'd make it quick.

"You can't be allowed to destroy anything else." Each step he took towards Vade felt like agony. "This is all I have to give you now. I'm sorry."

"Don't worry, little Dragon."

Althus froze—Vade's lips had moved, but the voice belonged to someone else. How? Was it some kind of Two-Voice that Althus didn't understand?

"So touching." Vade heaved forward, letting momentum throw him off the couch. He hit the linoleum floor with a smack and began to crawl towards Althus, dragging his legs behind him, his bones snapping and popping.

Why wasn't the poison working? For the first time tonight, his confidence left him. Whatever moved those lips wasn't the man he had spent so much time agonizing over.

"Who are you?" Althus asked.

Vade spoke Two-Voice faster than Althus had ever heard. The floor cracked and rumbled as black, boiling bubbles broke through. Vade lifted up his head from the floor and his eyes rolled back as thick, black mucus dripped from the corners of them. "Someone that does not like their vessel toyed with."

Fear hit Althus like a bucket of cold water, but he rushed forward with his blade, ready to pierce Vade through the heart. But instead he was repelled backwards, slamming hard into the wall. His whole world rattled.

"Foolish." Vade—Vade's body? Was he still in there?—
was getting to his feet now. Slowly, so the spell still held
some effect. Althus was too dizzy to take advantage but
Vade wasn't strong enough to attack yet either. "You use
my tongue and delude yourself into thinking you're some
master. You understand *nothing* of what I can do."

His tongue? Was this a demon possessing Vade's body?
Althus was out of his depth here. Had the demon been
in control this entire time? Maybe *this* explained how a
good man could do such evil. His heart wanted to save
Vade, but there were too many unknowns. All he had left
was his mission. Get the password, burglarize the Onyx
Cabin, and deal with whatever horrors he found there. He
had no other choice.

"You're making this a lot easier."

Vade threw his head back and laughed. "You're a
puppy yapping at a wolf. It's almost cute."

"*Eno eru gyan!*" Clarity and vitality jolted through him.

"Your accent is terrible," the demon said.

The demon's voice was *wrong*—it lacked all of Vade's
charming cadence. Althus wanted to rip it out of his
lover's throat.

"*Lia ghan tpa roa tet ctar!*" Althus summoned a spear of
light from his palm and hurled it towards Vade.

It was meant to be a distraction, but it struck Vade in
the shoulder. The other man wheeled backwards, crashing
through the glass table. Althus was surprised—the Vade
he knew would have easily dodged that blow. Perhaps the
demon didn't have full command of Vade's body?

"*Shun akari e'ma!*" the demon roared, as the entire VIP
room quaked. Gray chains rose out of the floor, burning
where they wrapped around Althus's wrists, ankles, and
waist. "You're special, Althus. Delectable. You deserve to
be savored." The demon licked Vade's lips.

Althus groaned as the chains continued to burn him.
"*Lagra vano!*"

His flesh became magma and burned through them. He punched Vade across the jaw. Again, the other man was too slow to react. The demon wasn't a Whisper, it didn't know how to fight. Althus followed up with a blow to the stomach and felt the sizzle of Vade's flesh on his knuckles. Before the demon could call on Two-Voice again, Althus tossed him over his shoulder and sent him crashing into the wall.

Someone *had* to have heard their commotion at this point.

It didn't matter. This had to stop *now*.

"Get up, you piece of shit," Althus said.

Vade held up a hand. "A bit beat up at the moment."

That wasn't the demon's voice. That was Vade. He'd found his way back. How? Relief and anguish swelled up in him in equal measure. Althus didn't know what to think. It would have been so much easier to kill the demon. "Vade? Is that you? I—"

Vade nodded, slowly and painfully, as he clutched his ribs and rose to his feet. Bewildered desperation shone in his eyes. "We really need to talk. I think—I think I might—no, I *know* I love you too."

# OLDERIANE — THE DISCORDANT HEART

VADE WAS FLATTENED by his own declaration. His heartbeat was louder than all the screams of people fleeing the club. But this was what had pushed his way past the demon's control. Vade wouldn't—he couldn't—deny what his heart told him: he loved Althus and he wasn't going to run from it anymore.

But he couldn't begin to fathom what it meant right now, as he and Althus stared at each other with haunted eyes and panting breaths. This wasn't how any of this was supposed to have gone. Vade had always planned on eventually making a clean kill, letting sadness briefly crush him, and then returning to the steady grind of his work. Instead, Althus had struck first and Vade would have been dead if not for the demon's intervention.

The demon wasn't gone, it was right beneath the surface. *Your lover has such fire. I want to extinguish it. His screams would make me quiver.*

How could they move past *that*?

Althus finally got his breathing under control. "You going to say something else or——"

"Like what? Should I suggest a nice sit-down dinner? Not sure what you're looking for here."

Althus balled his fists. "Did you mean it? Or are you just trying to save your life?"

Vade swallowed. "Meant every word."

"You had to wait till we're brawling it out to finally say it?" Althus's blood still ran cold at the thought of the demon snatching control of Vade. "And what *was* all that?"

Vade almost lied, but decided their way forward couldn't have that any more. "It's a demon, I think. It has to be. It's been there a while. I don't know, I thought I could keep it in line."

"In *line*! A fucking demon. So it *is* true. And what, you just thought you could pat its head and keep it in your mind all nice and quiet?"

"What do you mean it's true—nevermind. Look, listen. I just know I love you and I want to be with you."

Althus pounded his palms into his forehead a few times. "I can't be with a fucking *Whisper*. That goes against everything we stand for."

"But you think it's easy for *me* to give everything up for a violent rebel?"

Althus flinched. "Oh, so we're going there?"

"You just tried to kill me, so yeah we're going there."

Althus paced around the wreck of a room. "If I had killed you earlier, maybe Akjo and Taigan would be alive. You slaughtered them, didn't you?"

Vade remembered. Shame coursed through him. What had happened on Dyamii was—it still made him feel sick to remember the pleasure he'd found in that. "I had to kill them but not like—I didn't even know I could do that."

"As if that makes it better."

"And you've never had to do anything you didn't want to do as a Phantom Dragon? Or do you all just get off on blowing up factories with innocent people in them?"

"My country gave me a *weapon* and sent me to war when I was six," Althus reminded him. "I've got a long list of shit I wish I hadn't done, but I've never avoided responsibility for any of it."

"Deflecting. I'm not talking about you as a kid. You're a rebel *now*. Churches, hospitals, factories, missionary caravans. Groups like those don't mind collateral. Don't try to make mine seem worse."

"You are worse! I've seen the protocols, the paperwork, the experiments," Althus said. "We have a pulse on all the sick shit your government does. Even what they've done to—"

"And you're all just saints piously asking for change?" Vade asked, incredulous. "Riceno Park, 337 dead. Charliss Lake, 706 dead. I've seen what rebels do and the bodies you leave behind!"

"*We're* not like that. We're not. Why would *you* stay with people that would put a fucking demon in you?"

Vade's chest locked up. "What are you talking about?"

Althus blinked back at him. "What?"

"They didn't put the demon in there, it—" He struggled to get to his feet, his head feeling light. How else *had* it gotten there?

"It's true. Sa—one of my informants has evidence. I just put two and two together."

Vade's vision blurred. "Shut—"

The room spun and Althus shouted at him from what sounded like a great distance. Then there was nothing but the demon, its uproarious laughter overwhelming else. Vade pushed back against it with every bit of willpower he could muster—he couldn't allow the creature to get a hold of him again, not when Althus was still in here—but the demon wasn't trying to take control of his body this time—

*I don't want your pretty lover yet. Now that you know most of the truth, let's give him a look into all your precious memories… remember…*

—he was taking control of his *mind*. The demon uttered soft, diabolical words in Two-Voice, but Vade had no idea what they meant. His concentration was fleeting—he was being sucked down a wintry funnel. Remember what? Cold sweat dripped down his back. He could make out each individual drop in his mind. Remember what? He heard Desiree's voice, soothing him, telling him it would all be fine. Remember what?

The levy in his mind broke, followed by another squeal of laughter from the demon, his torturer. It all came rushing back. Vade clutched his chest…or was he watching himself clutch it? He couldn't be sure. Nothing felt real.

He was a boy, frail in frame with white pajamas and shaking hands. He'd been strapped down to a metal table and surrounded by older Whispers. They all wore crisp suits, eyes made sage by horrors they willingly inflicted and not a smile or drop of kindness among them. The room went black and harsh screams called out for a young Vade. The boy didn't—couldn't—answer. A cold wind swept through the shadows and over him, carrying the tiniest whisper of Cyn's voice.

"We have to do this. They'd want us to do this."

The screams eventually became his own. Desiree stood over him in a dark room full of long metal tables. She rubbed a hand gently along his hair as she talked to someone else outside of Vade's view. "Are you sure?"

"Yes, the demon is definitely embedded."

"Excellent. We'll see how long he holds out."

A young Vade whimpered. "It's going to eat me. It's a monster. Please." Vade hated how cold it was. He didn't want this. He wanted to stay the same.

"We don't fear monsters." Desiree leaned over him and put her hands on his shoulders. She leaned down and whispered in his ear, "I've never lied to you Vade. I promise. It will make you strong."

Vade rushed back into his body with every memory unfurled. The spool of his mind had been pulled and pulled until it was a pile of threads with no shape to them. The demon's laughter and the screaming shadows grew faint. Althus held him, panic writ across his face. Vade shook his head, trying to orient himself. He struggled for words at first. "They—didn't help me."

"I know. I saw, baby. All of it."

Too much had been unraveled in him. He gripped Althus closer and started to cry. "She put a demon in me. She did this. All of it."

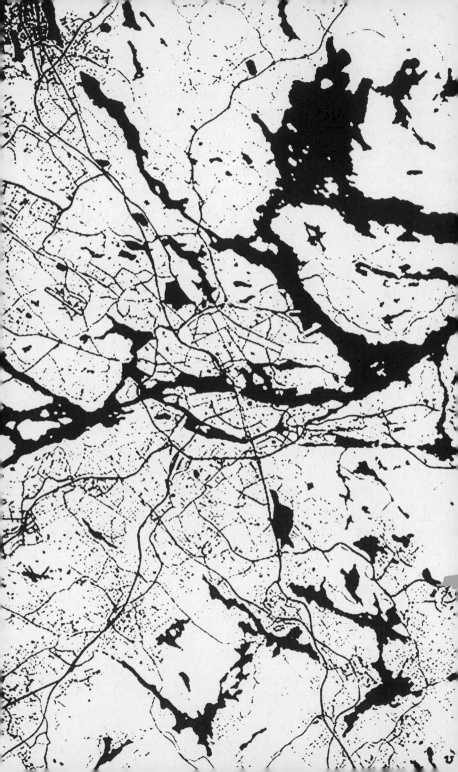

# OLDERIANE — THE DISCORDANT HEART

ALTHUS COULDN'T EXPLAIN it. One minute Vade
collapsed in his arms, and the next, he was pulled
into vision after vision from Vade's past. The factory
explosion that killed his parents and solidified Vade's
path to being a Whisper. Two broken orphans molded
into weapons. Desiree telling him that his sister had gone
missing and later that the Phantom Dragons played some
part in it. Every cruelty, every command, every murder,
every *blatant lie*—all wrapped in a guise of patriotism. It
disgusted and angered him to see what the Amos-Morbine
compact had done to him. To those children.

It made an awful sort of sense to Althus. Whispers were
capable of a chilling amount of casual violence.

"We have to go," Althus said, struggling to get Vade
to his feet. The Discordant Heart's security would be
here soon, favor or no, and Althus wasn't in the mood to
convince them they were just another pair of frightened
clubgoers. Vade's memories left Althus confused at best,

but after seeing them, he knew protecting the man wasn't committing some kind of sacrilege. "Get up, Vade. If you love me like you say, then you have to get up!"

Vade dragged his feet, gripped Althus' arm. "I tell you I love you and you say nothing?"

Althus winced and rubbed the back of his neck. Despite everything, he had been waiting to hear that for years. And now—nothing about this made sense. "We're literally going to die if we don't leave."

"Don't pretend you don't love me too."

The words had been sitting at the back of his own throat for just as long. "Of course I love you, you idiot, but I was supposed to kill you and run. I didn't, and now I have no idea what comes next."

"Back to the hotel," Vade said between pained gasps. "We can rest."

Althus almost argued—they needed to flee the city for their lives, not roll into a fancy hotel for a nap. But Vade wasn't in any shape to escape a metropolis right now. The festival would provide them some cover, so best to take advantage of it. He'd pass off Vade's injured slump as drunken stupor. "Alright. But we're going to need a plan soon, Vade. We can't hide forever."

Karmola's face flashed through his mind, fiery disappointment marring her features.

# OLDERIANE — THE TORAN DEEP

**V**ADE LOST TRACK of himself somewhere between the ravaged Discordant Heart and the Toran Deep. When his eyes opened, they revealed the mosaic on the ceiling of his hotel room: dragons with gold and white scales twisted and twined around each other, surrounding a bundle of Olderiané sugar cane.

His newly unlocked memories flooded him with information. The fight, the demon, the procedure. Desiree's gentle voice telling him it would all be okay. Even now, he wanted to believe her. Even now, he tried to work out some reason why the woman who had become a second mother to him would freely let a demon occupy his mind.

He felt Althus's eyes on him. Pain-stakingly, Vade cranked himself up on his elbow so he could look at his lover head on. The Phantom Dragon sat on the edge of the bed wearing only a towel, his tattoo was visible to him for the first time, a ghost-like dragon trailing from shoulder to elbow. Did Althus trust him now or had exhaustion set in?

The hotel room light glistened across the water droplets lingering on his shoulders. Beautiful as ever. Had everything Vade remembered at the Discordant Heart really happened? The events were like a fever dream, but one thing stuck out like a bright, burning star. One moment that made his breath catch.

"I was seven the first time I killed someone from the Compact," Althus said, almost out of nowhere. "Making it to ten seemed as impossible as finding my Dad and demanding to know why he'd sold me. Being thirty-two and here in this room with you—*this* is not a life I ever counted on."

Vade frowned and bit the inside of his cheek. "My parents were killed in a factory explosion caused by rebels. Terrorists. The place manufactured fungal ammunition, it was supposed to be an Enoch deterrent. Otherwise, I never would have become a Whisper. I never wanted any of this either."

"But at some point you really believed in it." Althus stated it as a fact.

Vade couldn't dispute it.

He'd believed in everything he'd done. Even when he felt annoyed, frustrated, or flat out disgusted with the Amos-Morbine Compact's hierarchies, he'd still been convinced of the better world it could create. One where kids didn't lose their parents to senseless violence. But that stubborn conviction had been anchored to Desiree. And now he knew intimately how little she thought of him. How to her, he was just a tool to be used and discarded.

"What made you finally decide I had to go?" Vade asked.

Althus looked away. "Who says that isn't still on the table?"

"You've had plenty of opportunities."

"I just—" Althus stopped, frustrated. "How the fuck did we get here?"

Vade looked back up at the dragons on the ceiling. "Because of lies. Lies we told ourselves. Lies others fed us.

All lies. I've wanted to walk away from all this a dozen times before now and just be with you. But Desiree—she's good at keeping what she wants close."

"The Onyx Cabin," Althus said, finally answering that question. "You have the password. I was sent to kill you and pull it out."

"People actually call it that, huh?" Vade smirked. "I can live with you wanting to kill me for that. You'd make me the greatest failure in Whisper history but at least it'd be worthwhile."

Althus finally turned to him, face twisted in anger. "And Dyamaii? You thought we had something to do with your sister so you were going to kill us all?"

Vade's instinct told him to dodge that blame, but he bit them back. "Yes. Cyn was all I had left. And when I found out she was gone forever, I needed someone to pay for that."

"And now?"

"My sister's dead. That hasn't changed. If it wasn't the Phantom Dragons, I need proof. You saw my mind. I wasn't getting off on it. I'm not a scumbag."

"The demon sure is." Althus's anger held. "Does it really matter? Two of my friends are dead. You can't just walk that back."

"But I *can* start making the right kind of difference. I can give us a life where we don't have to do this." Vade pressed forward, not giving Althus a chance to respond. "Desiree doesn't know what I know. I have the password to the Manticore Vault. I can give you rebels a chance to do some real damage." Vade reached over to take Althus's hand. "It will give us a chance to have a *life*. I'm not saying forgive me, but let me at least try to earn it."

Althus squeezed his hand. "We deliver the password first. We can talk the rest after."

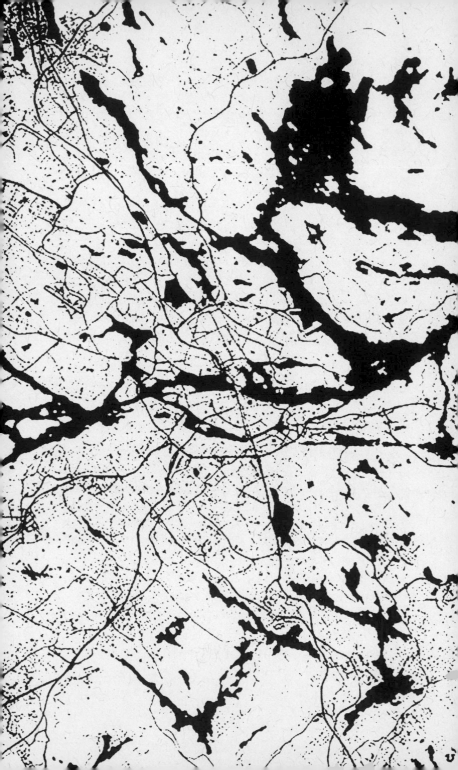

# OLDERIANE — ALL WOUNDS CLINIC

**T**HE SUN HADN'T yet come up when Althus pounded on
the door of Sajime's clinic. He knew he was risking
everything by bringing Vade, but the mission had been
to get the password to the Onyx Cabin. Vade would give
it to them freely. That had to count for something. Althus
needed this first step into a different life to not blow up in
his face.

Sajime flung the door open, her crystal monocle nearly
falling off her face. "What the fuck, Althus? You're not
even supposed to be here. Banging on my door like an…"
her voice softened and trailed off at seeing Vade, "…idiot."

"We need to talk. Inside preferably." Althus put a hand on
her shoulder to get Sajime to focus on him. "Please. Inside."

"What have you done?" Sajime's hands twitched,
caught between fear and violence. "Talk fast, Althus."

Althus saw the tension and hoped it wouldn't lead to a
brawl right here in the alley. He had faith this was the best
place to go. Sajime was a friend and convincing her would
be easier than Karmola.

"Karmola was wrong. Killing him was never going to get us in, but he's going to help us. I'm telling you, he's not with them."

Sajime narrowed her eyes. "What if he changes his mind?"

Althus knew she had just dealt with a potential turncoat in her network and he could only imagine the worst case scenarios going through her head now. He didn't have any clever way to put her at ease, he only had the truth. "I promise we're safe, Sajime. I'm asking you to trust me. Please."

There was a solid moment where they just stared at each other but Sajime relented and let them in. Right at the entrance, she made sure to have pictures of all the imperial leaders. Just in case there was a raid, she needed to give the appearance of loyalty. Althus knew it must pain her to have Prime Consort Jami staring at her every day knowing all the Phobeta Courts had done to her. He honestly looked like the kind of old man you would come to get advice from. Kind eyes, soft lips, and enough wrinkles to fool you into thinking they came from hard-won wisdom. But it had only been a lineage of cruel privilege that provided him with such longevity.

The clinic was busier than Althus had ever seen it as Sajime hustled them to the back storage. Most of the people writhing and moaning on her cots were younger Olderiane locals judging by the shell bracelets around their ankles and the buzzcut blue hair that had become a fad amongst the local youth. Many were wrapped in heavy blankets, their teeth shaking loud enough to create an awful sort of music.

"Imperial tourists bring their drugs right along with their money." Sajime aimed every word at Althus like they were darts. "Most of them will be fine. You'd better hope."

"Sajime—"

"You don't get to bring one of *them* into a safe space I spent years building and tell *me* how I can talk to him. Not a single word."

Her resentment saturated the air and Althus knew he'd
stretched the limits of their friendship. He hoped not to
the point of irreparable damage.

Sajime locked the door behind her. "When I was
in prison, the Paleskins treated us like rats to run
experiments on. They'd pick two or three of the newest
prisoners to befriend, give preferential treatment, the
whole works. They'd do it for two or three months, never
letting the rest of us say a word. The ones who did died
loud and painfully. They'd wait until—"

"I get it, Sajime." Althus stopped her, knowing that
running through those memories wasn't good for her. "But
this isn't a game. He's serious."

"He's a Whisper. I'm not taking any chances. I'm sedating
him."

Vade took a step back. "That won't be happening."

"You want me to barrel over every instinct I've built
for the last decade about these fuckers? Then he's going to
have to get damn uncomfortable." Sajime was ready for a
fight. Her nails were already glowing. "Either he takes my
paralytic or you two can get right the fuck out."

She was serious. Althus took Vade's hand. "I'm asking
her to trust us. It's gotta be reciprocated."

Althus wasn't sure where they would go if Vade rejected
this. But if he was serious about making things right then
it had to start here.

"Fine, but I need to see and hear everything."

"You will. I have plenty I want you to hear too."

She pressed her nails into Vade's cheeks. He winced as she
dug them in. Althus knew she didn't have to do that. The
veins in Sajime's hands bulged and turned cerulean as they
pumped poison into Vade's body; the reaction made him go
rigid. It didn't take but a few seconds but Althus squirmed.
Vade could have been a statue. Still breathing. Still alive.

"This is the part where you tell me why I shouldn't kick
your ass. And quick."

Althus took a deep breath. "What you learned about torture dimension experiments is real. Vade was one of them. He didn't know."

"Oh, so let me guess." Sajime rolled her eyes. "His little feelings are hurt that the people he murdered for didn't think to include him in their depravity. And now what? You just—buy his sob story like a bee desperate for any drop of honey?"

Althus flinched. "I'm not saying he's perfect. I'm saying he's not *with* them anymore and he's going to give us the password to the Onyx Cabin. Would you kill him for helping us?"

Sajime ran a hand down her face. "He must have used Two-Voice on his dick for you to be this stupid."

"There's more to it, Sajime. I'm not naive." Althus told her everything about the demon and how he'd shared Vade's memories. The manipulations necessary to make a good man believe horrible things were a path to a better world.

Sajime's blank face and folded arms never budged, but she did at least wait until Althus was finished. "It could all be a fucking trick, Althus. Whispers could be barreling their way here right now."

"I know what I fought." Althus knew the only admission that would get Sajime to listen. "I don't remember the last time I was that scared."

Her harsh stance melted away with each second until she let out a long sigh. "Fuck. I knew you coming here was going to be nothing but trouble. First Paleskins and now I got a fucking Whisper in my clinic. Did he tell you the password?"

"No. And it wouldn't matter anyway, the damn thing is tied to his intonation. He has to be the one to say it. Look, I care about him, Sajime. Crazy as that sounds. I'm going to keep him safe."

She sighed again. "This is stupid and I'm stupid for helping you. But we're family. We'll figure this shit out."

Althus knew not to hug her, but he damn sure wanted to.

"The password isn't going to stop Karmola from wanting his head and you punished though. There's going to be a limit to how much I can help you here." She looked over his shoulder at a still paralyzed Vade "I can set you up with some fake IDs and tap into some of my burner bank accounts. But you'll be on your own after."

"Naw, I'm not running away from this fight, Sajime. We have a plan."

Vade groaned as the paralytic started to wear off. Sajime walked back to him and scratched her nail against his cheek. The same large veins pumped a substance into him that brought the paralysis to an end. She stepped back nervously.

"You got Althus into a world of shit, so you better be good for your word."

Vade coughed hard, covering his mouth with a balled fist, until he could speak. "Considering you might have killed my sister and that I still let you make me a helpless target, we're past me needing to prove shit."

Sajime raised an eyebrow. "Sister? Someone lied to you. We don't murder civilians."

"She was a Whisper."

Sajime laughed. "Then someone *really* lied to you. You were going to be the first Whisper we ever took the head off of."

A memory sparked in Althus—a memory from Vade. "Desiree told you she went missing in Ikit right? Sajime, didn't we run into a Whisper there?"

"Years ago. Now that you mention it—" She examined Vade, zeroing in on his face. "The two of you have the same nose. That might have been your sister. We took off the minute we saw her. She turned one of our informants and tricked us into showing up at an abandoned building. Nearly would have killed us without Akjo sensing something was off."

"So then—"

"Your little precious government lied to you again. You might want to get used to that." Sajime sounded all too satisfied delivering that blow. "Our policy has always been to stay low and keep away from you killers."

Althus could see this spiraling into a dumb argument that they didn't need. "The Onyx Cabin will have answers Vade. We go there and—"

"Wait. Pause." Sajime took a step back. "You're both as high as my patients if you think you can take the Onyx Cabin together. Even when Karmola considered it, she only ever talked about it being something we took on with the—with another crew who had skills we don't have."

"And would a single one of those groups trust the Phantom Dragons if they knew we were working with a Whisper?" Althus asked. He and Vade had discussed the basics of this plan that morning. "We can do this. Vade knows the layout. We get in, we get what we all need, we distribute the information. And then you help Vade and me be able to disappear. Feels like a fair trade."

Sajime narrowed her eyes at Vade. "Oh, I really do not like you. You're stupider than a mermaid swimming in lava if you think—"

"We're doing it, Sajime. Be my friend and back the play."

She threw her hands up in surrender. "I'll get you out of the city!"

# AMOS-MORBINE COMPACT — ONYX CABIN

**S**AJIME LIVED UP to her word and gave them new documents and train tickets out of the city. Vade got them out of the country with two well-placed phone calls—his years as a Whisper had stacked up blackmail material on dozens of government officials. Promising to make some of that dirt go away got them where they needed to be. Sajime's fraudulent identification worked exceedingly well, even if it felt wrong to travel without his usual military status. Depending on a rebel for help was not something Vade ever counted on.

The Manticore Vault. The Onyx Cabin.

The blacksite nestled riskily within a suburb near their shared border with the Enoch Consortius. The populace were mostly educated people of modest wage, completely unaware of the dangerous information right at the heart of their blissful existence. The Onyx Cabin looked like any ordinary office building: four floors of neutral paint and large panes of tinted glass.

Vade rented a motorcycle as soon as they got within Compact borders and took back roads, Althus pressed against him the whole way there. Betraying his nation for some romantic notion of love felt insane. But he kept telling himself that this love was worth upending every viewpoint he had ever held; after all, his loyalty to the Amos-Morbine Compact had been built on nothing but lies.

The unearthed memories still felt distant, like they belonged to someone else. He had spent so much of his life with the hardest parts of his childhood cut out that being reintroduced to them now felt like meeting a stranger. The child who went through those things was him, but he couldn't yet feel that child's pain in his bones. His disgust came only from an objective place: children weren't tools and Desiree had decided to train them in one of the worst places in known existence. That was plain, no matter who it happened to.

They waited until nightfall before pulling into an empty lot a block away from the Onyx Cabin. Vade reiterated the part of the plan that Althus hated the most: "I go in. You wait here. I get out."

Althus huffed. "We'd be better together."

"Not on this. Speed is the key. I know this building. You would only slow me down. I should be back before anyone can call for back-up, but if that doesn't work then I need you here ready to go" Vade added something that he hoped would soothe Althus. "Be my protector out here. If anything goes wrong, you'll be my best chance."

Althus frowned. "What kind of trouble are you expecting?"

"There are secrets in the Onyx Cabin I'm not privy to. Everyone, for a lot of different reasons, would be all over the Compact's ass. Even the stuff I know about—we've assassinated at least six of the Phobeta Courts' generals, the toxic air in Owanissa is entirely our fault—would guarantee war. Exposing that information could upend the entire global political landscape."

"All this sounds like more reasons I need to go with you."

Stubborn, but it was cute. Vade shook his head. "Trust me, your man has this. Just be ready."

"The only thing I'm getting ready for is going in there with you. " Althus wasn't going to budge on this. "I did not drag my ass all the way here to just sit outside. Deal with it."

Vade could argue, but they didn't have time. The shift change was happening soon and if they missed that window this went from an operation requiring a scalpel to one needing a chainsaw. He didn't want to leave this place littered with bodies. That scenario still left him deeply uncomfortable. He knew now who he had served but he hadn't reached the place where he could deliver indiscriminate death down on them.

Was that really what kept him from bringing Althus? A Phantom Dragon certainly would have a different view on the preservation of life in this scenario. Didn't that mean some part of him was still thinking like a Whisper? The very part of himself he promised Althus he would let go of? Vade didn't break promises.

"You follow my lead on this completely," Vade said, ignoring Althus' smirk of victory.

*You're not ready, Vade.*

He ignored the demon's admonishment; it didn't know the strength of his resolve. He would break loose of his old ways and build a new life with Althus. Serving the Amos-Morbine Compact was firmly in his past. Cyn had talked about eventually getting assigned here. She'd seen it as the pinnacle of a Whisper's career, being entrusted with safeguarding the greatest secrets of the government. She'd always wanted to protect *something*. Whether it was him, or Desiree, or the whole Compact. The eternal guilt of not being able to save their parents. He hated how an event neither of them could control had been used to manipulate so much of their lives.

Well, that stopped tonight. Vade told Althus the plan, shushing him whenever he tried to interrupt, and after he finished, he kissed him, full and deep. "Needed to do that just in case."

"Oh fuck that," Althus said, holding out his wrists so Vade could tie them. "We're getting out of this. I didn't fuck up one of my favorite night clubs to fail here."

Vade smirked. It would be a long time before they got to party at the Discordant Heart again. "We get in, get the core and get out. The security here is minimal for appearances, but there are enforcement units, dozens of them, in close proximity. We can't take them all. Follow my lead, remember."

He brought him to the entrance, keeping a good grip on the back of Althus's neck. He might have squeezed a little harder than either of them would have liked, but that was part of the ruse. Vade just needed him to keep quiet. The rectangular glass security booth at the gate's entrance was unmarked but still utilized AMC standard communication gear—Vade would recognize that antenna anywhere. The guards were clad head to toe in black, lightly plated armor. They'd been trained to be agile, deadly, and quick to alert other nearby units of any incoming threats.

The guards stiffened at the sight of them. The Manticore Vault didn't just have people walk right up to the gate. Making Vade look like a prisoner was the only thing saving them from a barrage of knives turning them into blood faucets. Vade took advantage of their apprehension by not giving them time to think. "The storm makes the forest grow, but the fire keeps it tame." They relaxed upon hearing the password, so he pressed on. "Whisper designation 8951-Violet. Bringing in a prisoner for interrogation."

"No interrogations were scheduled today, sir," the young guard said. Starting with the password had taken most of the aggressive edge off. Now they were just playing games of procedure.

"This terrorist has information too sensitive to allow him to be detained anywhere else. Protocol 31-311." *Any properly verified Whisper can claim government space as mission critical.* Desiree required her Whispers to know the ins and outs of Amos-Morbine procedure. He had already provided the password and his designation. They shouldn't be able to turn him away, even if it *was* the Onyx Cabin.

The guard behind the security desk accessed her data core. Her eyes glossed over as she accessed the index. She set down the core and nodded to her compatriots. "Protocol 31-311 gives him clearance. Let him in."

"Continue with the shift change." A stocky guard with an ugly mustache pointed to Althus. "You got that thing in check?"

"I'm a Whisper." Vade didn't have to fake offense. What Whisper did he know that would bring in a prisoner that wasn't completely subdued? The insinuation alone made Vade want to give the man a dressing down.

The guard pointed to a blonde guard amidst his fellows. "You come with me. We'll bring them to the lobby and let Yemaia sort it all out."

They walked across the large parking lot towards the Onyx Cabin's main entrance.

Vade fought to stay relaxed. He hadn't counted on someone familiar being here, but it made sense. He avoided looking at Althus. These guards weren't suspicious but he wasn't going to get lax.

The stocky guard was speaking into a radio. "His Whisper designation is 8951-Violet. He's got a prisoner that needs to be interrogated here." A pause. "Understood. We're bringing him and the prisoner now."

"Yemaia's a colleague," Vade said. It would be suspicious to not mention it—she likely already had her own radio or access to the building's intercom system. Vade knew from his security run-throughs that the two systems were connected. With a quick hand movement, Vade unclipped the blonde guard's radio from his belt. "I'm sure she vouched for me."

"She did. She's as surprised as we are by the unannounced visit."

"It will be quite the orderly world when rebels decide to work on our schedule."

The guard grunted. "Fair enough."

During the walk, Vade kept close to Althus, sliding him the pilfered radio. They reached the lobby and waited for Yemaia. She had done him no wrong and had even been a friend to Cyn. As much as it bothered him, Yemaia would have to be dealt with.

"Didn't think I'd be running into Desiree's little favorite again so soon." Yemaia stepped out from the elevator at the far end of the lobby with a small group of security accompanying her.

"Favorite might be a stretch. But I do good work. Everything quiet here at the Vault?"

"Quiet enough." She jerked her chin at Althus. "This one of them?"

"Only reason I would even bother bringing him here."

"We should probably get in touch with Desiree. Give her an update. She might want to hear whatever this rebel has to say." She stared daggers at Althus. "Kind of glad you brought the scumbag here."

"So am I. Two voices are always better than one," Vade said, the words a signal to Althus.

The ropes binding Althus fell away. He whipped out the radio and summoned Two-Voice. "*Slanix eedaw'p!*"

Yemaia and everyone around them slumped to the ground. Everyone who Althus's words should be asleep for a few hours.

"You stuck to the plan," Vade said, pleased.

"Alright, that brought us some time," Althus said, rolling his eyes. "Where's that data core?"

"Tenth floor."

Althus cracked his knuckles and shook out his hands.

"Let's grab the thing and be gone before these assholes wake up."

Vade was silent during the elevator ride to the tenth floor. There really was no turning back now. Vade sat with that alone, not wanting to make Althus worry about his resolve.

The elevator opened directly to the tenth floor control center, which held tight rows of translucent pillars twined with electric cords that blinked blue and white. The cords flowed beneath the translucent floor. In the center, the core sat atop a black pyramid-shaped console. The entire floor buzzed loudly from all the power being fed into it.

"Is that it?" Althus asked.

"Stay here."

Vade approached the core, cautious of the facility's schematics, sure some trap would be activated or that someone would come out from behind one of the pillars to tackle him. Why would this room be unguarded, considering the asset held here? He paused, assessing himself and the room. Were any slow-acting or hidden Two-Voice effects at play here? It might be paranoia, but paranoia kept him alive. When nothing happened, caution gave way to a hungry and immediate curiosity. This device could tell him right now what happened to Cyn. There was time...

He splayed his hand against the spherical core and nearly fell forward as his palm became plastered to its surface. The veins of his hand turned red and a warmth crawled up Vade's arm to spread across his chest. The heat made him calm, too calm for a situation where people could come charging in ready to attack at any moment. Vade didn't fight the feeling. The core rattled and eased its grip, but not enough for Vade to pull away. Far away screams echoed in the back of his mind— unsurprising, if the core's internal security had been been constructed with Two-Voice.

The demon sighed in satisfaction at hearing its native tongue. *Your race is admirable in its cruelty.*

Vade couldn't respond because in that moment, the core and all the information it contained opened up to him.

The core knew what he wanted without him having to think it, drawing his mind down an endless hallway marked with an infinite stretch of glowing green doors on both sides. Each door had a combination of letters and numbers embossed on it. Vade walked, not on his own, to one labeled 0219N0621. The door opened and the image shifted to Cyn at a debriefing: straight-laced, wearing a suit, with her hair pulled into a ponytail. The image shattered like glass and was replaced with a giant stack of papers being shuffled madly. That image shattered too, replaced with a row of pages floating in blackness, PROJECT PEAK emblazoned across each of them.

He didn't need to read anything. The core fed him the information like a stiff drink. The demon laughed as the knowledge was imparted on it too.

*This woman willingly brings more of my kind here. Her arrogance is astounding. She understands so little.*

Vade wasn't the only Whisper with an unwelcome guest. There were dozens of Whispers, Cyn among them, who'd had demons fused to them. Project Peak took it a step further. Instead of one demon, she was attempting to fuse multiple ones to a single Whisper in order to create a Two-Voice user that could access any part of the torture dimension's language. To create soldiers with no limits on the power they could call upon.

The truth was right in front of him: Cyn had volunteered for the project and died in the earliest stages of it.

More than the horror of Cyn's death, what sickened him more was that Desiree had succeeded. The Peaks were real and according to the core, seven of them would be deployed at the Opal Conference.

"I imagine you're a bit…angry." A voice that sounded like five speaking at once called out from beside Vade. He turned to regard a bulky dark-skinned man in a slate uniform he didn't recognize.

"Angry doesn't begin to cover it. Tiangu, I take it?" Knowledge from the core still flooded him. There wasn't time. "Baby, I need you to take the core and get out of here."

"If you think I'm leaving you against whatever the fuck that is—" Althus reached his side. "—you've chewed some bad worms."

Even in the midst of this awful turn of events, it felt good to have someone refuse to leave his side.

"Protocol says I should have killed you before you accessed it. But it seemed fitting for you to see how weak your sister was before you follow in her footsteps." The Peak's impeccably white grin pissed Vade off more.

Vade saw the ploy for what it was. The bastard wanted to enjoy this all alone.

"My demons protected me from that little trick you pulled downstairs." The Peak cracked his knuckles. "They're ready for me to rip your head off and feed it to the maggots already munching on Cyn."

Vade would kill him for that, but not now. The core was important and his best path to getting justice for Cyn.

*"Spara eeina'd." "Fihu stang." "Boxar nelk."*

The Peak spoke all three phrases simultaneously. The anger Vade felt yielded to cold panic. It was one thing to know Desiree had created a weapon this powerful and another thing entirely to see it in action.

*"Lidar ghari't!"* Vade touched the core, making the orb much lighter and easy to grab. He tossed it to Althus—

And an enlarged, bone-covered fist punched Vade in the shoulder and sent him wheeling through the air.

Vade cracked hard against a pillar. He slid down it, head spinning. He wouldn't be able to move fast enough to dodge a second blow.

While Vade's thoughts were still muddled, the monster barrelled at him with locomotive speed, but Althus jumped in front of him. He held up the core. The Peak came to a complete halt, unwilling to destroy the Amos Morbine Compact's most prized possession.

The brief hesitation allowed Vade to get to his feet. *"Fawa styi ergost!"* He grabbed Althus around the waist and sprinted towards the window, ignoring the protests of his wounded body. Three dislocated fingers, maybe a broken shoulder, and definitely two broken ribs gave him a lecture on limits even as he barreled through glass and into open air. The skyline opened up to them as they crashed through. He clutched both Althus and the core with everything he had as they tumbled through the sky.

This wasn't the kind of victory he wanted, but at least it'd be a painless death. And the core would be destroyed. He could leave the world knowing that at least.

Vade closed his eyes, waiting for the end.

A roaring dragon interrupted all his thoughts of doom and anger. It sounded exactly like he'd imagined, primal and majestic. A cold wind rushed over him as he fell onto the phantom dragon's transparent bulk and into the solid arms of Althus. It felt like being in the eye of a hurricane, alongside twenty monstrous feet of concentrated fury.

"You better have a good reason for dragging me out of a damn window," Althus complained. "It was just one Whisper—"

Stubbornness. That quality had pulled through and saved both of them. White wisps of smoke circled all around them as they flew through the sky. It really was a phantom dragon. Vade couldn't believe it.

Vade tried to speak through the delirium of blood loss and broken bones caused by the Peak's singular blow. "Desiree insane. Opal Conference, go. Go…faster."

The world slipped away from him, but before it went completely black the demon spoke again:

*Oh! Your mind is all mine now. Your dreams—yes, let's unveil your fears.*

A DESOLATE PLAIN that never seemed to end. Air that reeked of burning oil. Ground like old, calloused skin, cracking with every step. Fissures that gave way to puddles of thick, purple liquid that bubbled and hissed, each bubble bursting to let out a tiny, brief shriek.

Clouds blanketed the sky, orange light filtered through them. No one knew if this place had a sun or not. The clouds had never parted, but large, monstrous shadows sometimes flitted above them. Some thought an entire legion of beasts lived in the sky, held back by something no one could explain. The only evidence of their existence were the rare bones scattered across the flat landscape.

Against a screaming wind, he ran after the other three children. "Cyn! Abel! Karmola! Wait up!"

After…what she did to him…Desiree still made him do physical training with the others here. It was another test. If they could complete PT in the torture dimension, they'd be better Whispers. Cyn wanted to be the best, and Vade wouldn't leave Cyn, so he would be the best too.

Cyn had no patience for him. "Keep up, Vade."

The cold air prickled his skin, and the desolate landscape of orange rocks and red sky felt like an unheeded warning. Humans weren't meant to be here. The wind screeched with a thousand violent voices in words he struggled to understand.

Whenever the training felt too much, Desiree told them, "Pain is the one beast that is guaranteed to weaken. You strike at its heart with every step forward." So Vade kept up.

"This place will literally eat you if we don't stick together," Karmola said.

He didn't need the reminder. The number of candidates grew smaller with every PT drill.

"Don't scare him, Karmola," Abel said. "Don't scare me either."

"Let's go." Cyn was exasperated. Vade had no idea how she wasn't terrified. "We find a sample and we get out."

"Why does she want a sky bone anyway?"

"It doesn't matter," Cyn said. "Desiree told us to get it, so we will."

"We're called Whispers, not parrots. Can you try and think for yourself at least once?" Karmola was always irate with them.

"Or I could simply rip your tongue out and never have to hear a question from you again." The voice wasn't Cyn's. Vade felt even more afraid.

They walked until memory blurred. The landscape melted into a swirl of red and orange before his mind brought him to a solid place again.

"We're never finding any." Karmola put her hands on her knees. "I swear I'd rather just run away."

"Don't let Cyn catch you saying that," Abel warned, then turned to Vade. "And don't you say a word."

Vade stuck his tongue out. He was sick of getting teased.

The ground shook beneath them and they exchanged wide-eye stares. Silence followed the shake, but that wasn't reassuring. Quiet in a dimension of screams was only a portent for horrible things.

Abel's mouth trembled. "We should—"

The ground erupted beneath Abel's feet as dozens of rocks shot up from the dirt, glowing green and orange, creating a jagged cloud around the boy. Vade rushed to Cyn's side, protecting his face and grabbing her hand tight. Abel cried out as the rocks collapsed. Vade winced as bones crunched and Abel's blood splattered across his face.

Vade, Cyn and Karmola didn't move. They couldn't. They were all going to die. Vade was going to be eaten.

The demon wouldn't let Vade look away. *He wasn't worthy. Neither are you. But if this is to be my prison, I will make you strong!*

Before Vade could dissent, the purple cloud swallowed him. Cold seeped into him as his vision went dark and a hungry shadow made itself at home in his flesh.

"Yes, this will do," the cloud said. "All this doubt and fear. What a feast." The warmth became a searing, unbearable heat. "Scream for me, child."

*Fight back Vade! If you want my power, you will fight back!*

Vade wasn't strong enough. He screamed and screamed.

When he woke up, the demon didn't speak for a very long time.

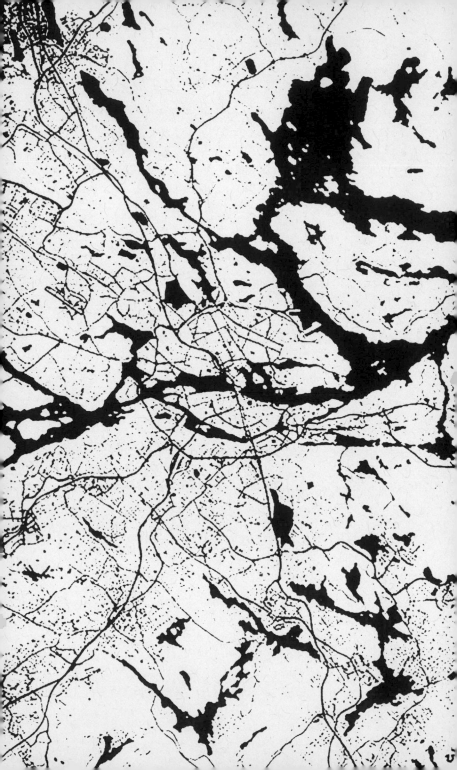

# VAZABA — SAFEHOUSE

ALTHUS WAS DESPERATE. Reaching out to Sajime was all he could think of.

They had hidden in the basement of a safehouse beneath an eccentric bookstore on the outskirts of Vazaba, a Compact city only a day's ride from the Onyx Cabin. Vade had been unconscious for more than twenty four hours and Althus's vocal chords were still sore from drawing out the phantom dragon. Calling the ancient beasts was a huge risk. The tattoos were implanted with all three dimensional magics, and the Phantom Dragons were never sure of their potency.

"We'll need to run tests." Sajime stood over Vade who'd been laid across a metal table and strapped down. Sajime's recommendation, even though it made Althus itch. "What the fuck happened in the Onyx Cabin? I can't believe you summoned the phantom dragon."

"Do you see what that Whisper did to him? He'd be dead if I hadn't."

"Okay, let's run through what we know." Her voice
had taken on the flat, objective tone Althus imagined she
used in her clinic. "You went in, he accessed the core but
then got his ass beat. You managed to escape from the
Amos Morbine Compact's most secure location using our
greatest secret. And now he just won't wake up. You're
sure that data core is inert?"

"I had to call you. I didn't know what else to do."

She nodded, some sympathy finally leaking into
her expression. "Honestly, I don't have a clue where to
start. He's banged up badly. I can help with the physical
injuries, but I don't think it has anything to do with why
he won't wake up."

Althus agreed. Vade had been babbling like a madman
during their flight. Something deeper had happened,
something more than a few cuts and bruises.

Sajime pressed her fingertips against the sides of Vade's
face. "I can trigger a reaction that'll make his body feel
like it's in extreme danger. Might be enough to wake him.
But are we sure we want to do that, given his friend?"

"The demon?"

"Yes, the fucking demon. I'm not in the mood to fight a
native of one of the worst places in existence."

"I'm not sure if we have a choice. Vade is the only one
that can tell us how to use that thing." Althus gestured
at the core. "I tried but I don't know how to navigate the
mind palace it projects me into."

"I can't make any promises."

Althus was beginning to let go of any idea that this
might end neatly. He felt like a fly trying to bring down an
eagle. It had seemed thrilling at first, the idea they might
succeed and throw the whole world into chaos. Now he
wondered if just running away made more sense. Maybe
they'd only have a few good years before their pasts
caught up to them, but it was starting to feel preferable to
a suicide run.

"If the demon shows up, I can wrangle it long enough for you to get out." There was a risk that using Two-Voice again right now might silence his voice permanently, but he had dragged his friend too far into this already. He couldn't let her put her life on the line.

"Before you start talking, let me do my thing." Sajime's black nails glistened and the veins in her hand became a shiny obsidian. She pressed her fingertips deeper into Vade's cheeks as painful yellow and orange blisters appeared along the top of her palms.

Vade's body jerked and his mouth cranked open. The slightest black mist flowed out as his hands flexed and his head darted around the room. Vade's eyes were wide open and intense. Sajime nodded. "He's up. Do your thing."

*"Rema vedin aldom yogu urmaja indo teli ntog ioza'n."* Sajime only heard, "You have your own music. Just let it play." He caught her smirking. If this worked, he'd ask her why later.

In the state Althus was in, each word required slow, careful pronunciation. That had never really been his forte, but sharing Vade's memories changed things. He handled Two-Voice differently now, like a part of Vade resided in him. And as each syllable was completed, it felt like Vade fell further into him. His faint cologne became a strong, immutable fragrance. But something was different this time. Althus also felt a rising sense of anger and sadistic delight, bubbling black ooze creeping into his thoughts. He'd latched onto two minds instead of one.

As soon as he had equilibrium, Althus asked the minds in his thrall, "What do you want?"

His mind split in two as he received both visions at once.

Althus was in Vade's body, looking down at his own head cradled against Vade's chest. Water splashed at their feet and the sun beamed down on them. Their shared heartbeat thrummed in his ears—Vade wanted a life with him.

Althus was also the demon—a living cloud of purple gas and blinking white lights that surrounded him as he lay on a desolate mountainside of cold orange rock. He felt the demon's desire as it caressed his unmoving, hypnotized body. He felt the demon's giddiness as it tried to open his—

Althus wrenched back from the vision, the backs of his hands itching; he hadn't expected such clarity. The last time he had performed the spell and asked this question, the target had delivered him a host of jumbled images. Nothing with a clear answer. Although, that target had been dead.

But the demon wasn't done with him. *I could show you the extremes of pain and pleasure, until you see the beauty of both.*

"I don't want anything to do with you or your sick ass dimension."

*But you already do. With every spell you speak. Where do you think those ghostly dragons you summon come from? They may wander many universes, but those great beasts share my home.*

"Give me back Vade or—"

*Or you can simply join us. Let me love and protect you as I have loved and protected him. I saved him on Dyamaii.*

"Fuck you. You were saving yourself." Within the demon's cloud, he saw a trembling child. It had to be Vade. Perhaps if the demon was distracted—he forced himself to sound genuine. "How do I know you can really love anyone?"

*What is love if it first doesn't begin with the self? Let me love you, Althus. You'll see…there is so much more to experience. I will elicit pleasure from every orifice you have, down to your very pores, and then I'll—*

With the same speed he used to rush battlefields as a child, Althus dashed into the demon's purple cloud and snatched Vade from within it. The demon roared.

He ended the connection and dropped to his knees. Sajime rushed to him but he held up a hand. "I'm okay. Is Vade—"

"Conscious. Not moving alot or speaking, but he's awake..."

"The demon wants to fuck me."

Sajime laughed. "That's all you figured out?"

"I don't know how Vade hasn't gone insane with that demon in there."

Althus had never doubted the use of his magic before. He knew its origins weren't kind, but he had never thought of them as fundamentally evil. But seeing what the demon wanted to do to him and how it spoke so proudly of Althus using Two-Voice...he was afraid now.

Vade groaned from the table. "Cyn. Karmola...are you ok? Abel's dead. He's dead."

Althus knew one of those names well and judging by Sajime's screwed up expression, she was thinking the same thing. Why was Vade calling out for Karmola?

"What did you just say?"

"I remember now." Vade spoke with more clarity this time, as he struggled against the bonds Sajime had placed upon him. "She was one of us. Your Karmola was a Whisper."

*By Chesryah.*

Althus waited in the warehouse alone.

The last time Althus had felt this angry was when he got news of Akjo and Taigan. He wasn't sure how many more angry thresholds he could pass. The world had always been a struggle for him, but at least it was usually a fight he recognized. Being with Vade had wrecked all the previous definitions he had held of the world. People he thought he could trust, people he let himself love...was anything worth believing?

*By Chesryah.* It was a phrase that all Phantom Dragons had agreed to respect. Whenever that phrase was invoked, you did what had to be done with no questions asked.

Althus had invoked it to bring Karmola here. He wasn't
sure if his status as a Phantom Dragon was in question,
but he was pissed off enough to try anyway.

Chesryah reminded them their fight wasn't over as long
as one fire still burned, whether in someone's heart or in
their hand.

Althus had asked Karmola to meet him in a warehouse
a day's travel away from Vazaba. The building was
functionally empty but often served as a meeting place for
a local rebel group Althus had formed a bond with. He
hadn't told them everything, but they trusted him enough
to give him the space for tonight.

"You could have chosen somewhere that didn't smell
like fish," Karmola said, her clicking heels announcing
her presence before her voice. "You know I hate fish."

He definitely knew. "Best place I could find."

Karmola stalked into the room, hiding her survey of
the space with a flip of her hair. She wanted to be casual,
but Althus knew her tells. She'd been the one who'd taught
him how to assess a room. Maybe he should be offended
that she didn't trust him, but given how mad he was, he
didn't trust himself to not just pummel her. The hypocrisy
reeked as much as the fish.

He sat on a dusty shipping crate, when she finally
settled down. "You seem nervous."

"Yeah, well, none of us should go throwing around
Chesyrah's name. If this is about your little Whisper crush—"

"You mean your former colleague."

The slightest flinch, followed by a long silence. Karmola
could keep a "fuck you" face going till the sun gave out.
Her guilt was solidly confirmed when she relented before
he did. "That was a long time ago."

"Really?!" Althus exploded. "That's it? That's all you
got! *A long fucking time ago.* Seriously?"

"I was a different person. I was a child."

Althus couldn't imagine clenching his fists any harder.

"No one is doubting your credentials, Karmola. We all know you're down for the fight, alright? But you didn't think it was a good idea to tell me that Vade—that my *target*—was someone you used to roll with?"

Karmola shrugged, displaying a level of nonchalance she couldn't be feeling. "It didn't matter. I saw an opening and I encouraged you to take it. Why speak on a past no one knew about but me?"

"Because I thought we were friends. Because I thought the Phantom Dragons were a family. Because a lie of omission is still a lie."

"What family you know doesn't have its share of secrets?" Karmola laughed, rich and deep like always. "Look. I wasn't trying to manipulate you or play at some secret agenda. I just wanted to put it behind me. That time of my life was…awful. You weren't supposed to fall in love with the guy. Besides, the last time I saw him in Obuss he had no idea who I was. So what happened?"

"Bomb ass sex," Althus joked. He could hear the sincerity in Karmola words; it cooled his anger.

She rolled her eyes. "Cute. But you've put us in real danger here, Althus. Really, what happened?"

"I wish I was joking." Althus told her a little more about Vade's memories, and the demon's role in that. "So we made a move on the Onyx Cabin."

Karmola sucked her teeth. "That's a move we should have all made together."

"And I'm supposed to believe you would have been okay with working at the direction of someone you wanted me to kill?"

Karmola's gaze flicked upward and she shook her head. "You could have gotten us *all* killed. If they captured you, we would have gone after you. We both know how that would have ended. And you showed them a dragon. They shouldn't know we can do that. Isn't it enough that we lost Akjo and Taigan?"

He refused to deal with that here. "Look, Desiree has a new toy. She's calling them Peaks and they can speak Two-Voice three times at once. She's introducing them at the Opal Conference. The other empires are going to escalate."

"And your solution?"

"Make the Opal Conference a big ass graveyard. Be the big change we've always been talking about."

"Trying to take the Opal Conference is incredibly stupid." But Karmola couldn't help but grin through her admonishment. "You know that, right?"

"Yea. Loud and clear. But I have to try. We have to try."

That grin vanished and became a tight line. "That *we* is doing a lot of work, Althus. Who are you including in it?"

"You owe it to him."

Karmola scoffed and pointed at herself. "I don't owe him a damn thing! He could have left, the same as me. He stayed right there, sucking Desiree's tit."

"The way he tells it, you just vanished one day. How did you avoid getting one of those things shoved into you anyway?"

Karmola looked away, paused and then exhaled. "I spoke Two-Voice better than most. Desiree wasn't ready to risk me until she saw how it worked long term with other candidates."

Althus whistled. "So you were privileged and used that to slip right on out."

"Oh come on! You're being ridiculous."

"I'm just saying…he could have used you the same way I did."

"Ree-dic-ulous!" She rolled her eyes. "I can't believe this is the angle you're working."

"Am I succeeding?" Althus could barely contain his smile.

"Only because I believe you didn't know those two were here with you."

Althus frowned. "Fuck me. You're kidding. Where?"

"Right here." Vade emerged from behind the dusty crates with Sajime. "You really didn't think we'd stay behind, did you?"

"I at least thought *she'd* have the sense to listen to me."

Sajime cackled. "Like I want to be left alone with a Whisper."

"It's been a while," Vade said to Karmola.

Karmola snorted. "You better be worth this." Althus knew it was the closest to an apology Vade would get. The idea that she even thought he could be *capable* of worth was a concession.

Vade nodded. "Messar. Can you get us in? After the Onyx Cabin, it's almost a guarantee any contacts I have there are burned."

Karmola looked him up and down. Calling it a critical eye would have been polite. "A fucking Whisper. Tuh. The Phantom Dragons will help this little love affair. We can get you into Messar."

Sajime gave Karmola a playful slap on the shoulder that earned her another dagger glare. "We were getting him there anyway. Vote was already decided. Just wanted you not to be a complete grouch about it."

*By Chesryah.* They were going to do what needed to be done. Althus hoped it'd be for the last time.

# MESSAR — ELAYNE'S CAGE

THE LAST TIME Vade had gone through the Hamarind Provinces on Amos Morbine Compact business, he'd gotten stabbed by a rebel. He hadn't expected to be back some time but the Phantom Dragons made sure to keep that last visit quiet as they traveled through the vast desert tunnels beneath the country. The two-day trek to Messar left Vade impressed with the Phantom Dragons' tenacity. There was something to be said for their ability to keep surprising the the empires. Eventually, he would have to start chipping away at his old ways of thinking if he wanted to be something different than a tool of the Amos-Morbine Compact.

*Ahh but such a delectable past. So much want, abandonment, and pain. There was a time I could have feasted forever.*

The demon didn't speak with as much force as it once had, but it was still more talkative than Vade would like.

The Phantom Dragons had set up camp at a state-licensed brothel of all places, the last place he'd go looking for rebels. Seemed like too obvious. Vade supposed he was slightly scandalized, despite himself.

Althus and the others were waiting for him in a room seemingly dedicated to various whips. He swore a few of them could be used in combat. They had pushed together the room's platforms into one large square and everyone had plopped down somewhere. He nodded to Karmola and sat beside her on a bench covered in buckles.

"Vade, can you tell us what you know about what we'll be dealing with at the conference? Would love to hear your perspective." Karmola sounded like that was absolutely the last thing she wanted from him. He couldn't say he exactly wanted much from her beyond a successful mission.

Whatever her reasons, she had left him with a demon stuck inside him. By Althus's account, she'd pushed more than any other for him to be killed. There weren't many reasons to give a shit about the woman.

"The empires keep the Opal Conference so low profile for a reason. If everyone knew the degree to which they cooperated and negotiated with one another, it would shatter the illusion of a world on edge." Vade understood more and more the part he had played in maintaining that illusion. "They need the world to believe that they're moments away from tearing each other apart so their peoples can be kept docile."

"It's always been a game with them," Karmola agreed. "Getting people to see that has been one of our hardest struggles."

"In this case, their game might be the only reason we're able to pull this off," Vade said. "Because they want this to be a thing that exists only in rumors, no one brings a large military presence and there will be minimal security. They don't want attention and they're arrogant enough to think they won't ever be found out."

Sajime huffed. "I still think we should have brought some of the other more organized movements in on this. They have resources we're sorely lacking."

Vade smirked, wondering how many of those groups would have wanted to kill him on sight. "Large troop movements will be noticed. We need to be as discreet as the empires are. That's how we get in and that's how we take them out."

"When you say *them*, just who are we talking about?" Althus asked.

"President Koo, Her Luminous Natalis VI, and Prime Consort Jami are all here."

Sajime elbowed Althus. "This has officially moved past saving your little love affair."

Karmola bit her bottom lip, hopping off the bed fortress to pace the room while everyone else watched. Vade didn't have a problem ceding her attention for a moment. He had more to say, and a little delay would keep him from getting yelled at. She finally stopped pacing and looked somewhere between mortified and in awe. "If we pull this off, everything changes. Really changes."

Vade wanted this to succeed more than anyone else, but that success also depended on making sure large doses of reality were delivered. "Don't take my previous statements to mean this will be easy. The security may be minimal, but it will still be the absolute best each empire has to offer."

"Don't worry. The poor little rebels can put up a fight," Sajime said.

"If I thought for a moment you couldn't, I would have left already." Vade hoped the statement could put a nail in the snark and animosity. Cooperation would be key to their success. "I can say, having once been on the other side, the Phantom Dragons have more than earned their name. But I know how my people think. More importantly, I know how Desiree thinks."

"We're listening, Vade." Althus cut his eyes at Sajime and until she grumbled her commitment. "Promise."

Vade nodded, grateful. "The conference takes place this year at the Eye of Messar. It's considered the cultural center of the Hamarind Provinces. The entire building is an ode to luxury and excess. A good cover to make something look like a gathering of your typical wealthy elite."

"I've procured you all attire that'll make us look the part. You're going to hate me, Sajime." Karmola smirked. "You have to wear heels."

"You've *got* to be fucking kidding me."

Karmola sprinkled a little more salt on the wound. "And it's an uphill walk."

"I'm suddenly kind of fine with just letting the empires win at this point."

"Once we're close," Vade continued, "Althus will use Two-Voice to make sure no one can remember our faces. We'll slip in after Karmola and Sajime create a distraction."

"When we're inside, everyone is going to be panicky and scrambling. I thought the point was to ice everyone at once?" Sajime pressed her lips. "There's not enough of us to start hunting season."

She wasn't wrong, but again, he knew these people in ways they couldn't. "None of them trust each other and none of them will want to lose face either. They may cooperate more than most know, but they are not allies. The distraction will make them congregate because they'll believe another is behind it and they'll want to make it clear they don't fear anything from each other. I can assure you they won't split up and sequester themselves. Their pride and egos won't let them."

"And we win? Just like that?" Sajime was not easy to convince.

"Nothing's promised. But they'll be on edge and we can use that. Corner them and do what has to be done," Vade said. "Our biggest advantage will be in the ways you have found to combine and utilize the dimensional magics in completely unique ways. The empires will destroy each other before they ever decide to cooperate. This will put things in our favor."

Karmola broke into a tiger's smile. "We have three Two-Voicers here. Not quite a choir, but they'll hear us just the same."

They continued reviewing the various operational details and Vade found himself invigorated by the rhythm of the planning. The Opal Conference would be the fight of his life, but for the first time he was grateful to have the Phantom Dragons at his back.

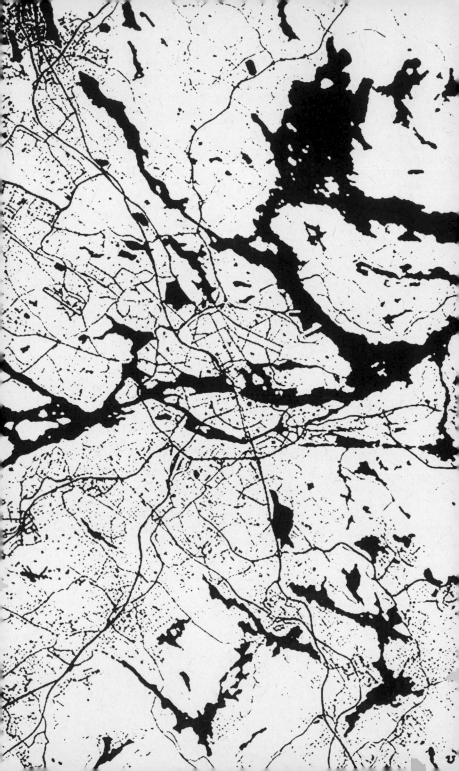

# MESSAR — THE OPAL CONFERENCE

MESSAR WAS A shield for the wealth of the empires. Their laws allowed avoidance of the dues and taxes that the empires demanded. Ironically, many of the people availing themselves of Messar's shielding had a hand in creating those very taxes and dues, but they had never intended to pay themselves. Althus hated Messar. It was disgusting proof that power was the truest currency. His skin crawled looking at every brick that had built up this decadent, hideaway country.

The capital had been designed as a series of rings placed inside each other. The largest ring contained Elayne's Gate and the necessary undesirables of the city. Each subsequent ring was higher in elevation and held people and businesses better regarded by society, until you reached the Eye of Messar in the center. The Phantom Dragons and Vade changed into their disguises halfway through the rings so as not to rouse suspicion.

If they played their cards right, they would just seem like a group of bureaucrats scrambling their way up the imperial ladder. Stupid. Althus hated the singing and dancing that politics put people through.

"They held last year's conference in Arodes Dali. The Enoch Consortius spent the whole time complaining about the amount of pet caracals the citizens had. Bad omens they claimed."

That sparked a memory for Althus. "Tinhadin and his crew got wiped out there that year. Was that—"

"It was. They got too close to things they shouldn't have."

He had never heard of the Opal Conference prior to Vade's disclosure. Althus thought the Phantom Dragons already had leads on every dirty secret the empires tried to bury, but he was wrong. Althus should have known the depravity never really ended.

"Ease up there. You look like you're ready to punch the first thing you walk into," Karmola whispered to him. Normally, that would have been a jibe, but today there was only cold seriousness in her words. The Phantom Dragons were used to operating in the shadows—it wasn't as easy for a giant to step on a fly if it was pitch black. But right now they only had their expensive suits as camouflage.

"This whole place reeks."

"Too many humans in one place tends to do that," Vade said.

Odd comment, but Althus couldn't disagree with it.

"Act your part and we'll have a chance to rid the world of the stench," Sajime said. "Smile a bit, too. If I have to walk around in heels, it's the least you can do. You'll spook someone if you don't calm down."

Her complaining about shoes was enough to get a smirk out of Althus. Still, the idea of not lashing out at these people wrapped in their comfort struck him as cowardly.

"We're close to the dome," Vade said, at the head of their group. He watched the crowd, made it look casual as always.

The negotiations that made up the bulk of the Opal Conference would be taking place beneath a domed structure called the Eye of Messar. It was a beautiful, cobalt colored jewel of architecture, accessible only to the moneyed and class elite. The excess made Althus want to hurl. Whole towns could be rebuilt, and every family in them fed, with the money just one of these rooms had in them.

With the building now clearly in sight, the operation could begin. There was a danger in using Two-Voice out in the open like this. A Whisper could be in the crowd, disguised as one of the decadent Messar citizens. But the Phantom Dragons needed to be close enough to make sure the spells worked exactly as planned. They lingered in front of a row of small shops right outside the Eye of Messar.

Vade tapped his forefinger against his thumb twice to signal them to begin.

*"Sela enik ofu acud'e."* Althus caressed Vade's cheek as he said it—anyone listening would have heard him promise Vade a nice night out in a week. Now their faces would fade from memories for the rest of the day. More than long enough to get in, get out, and laugh all the way to the nearest resort about screwing these bastards.

Sajime put a hand against the brick shop wall and closed her eyes. She wore gloves, but Althus was sure her veins were bulging and discolored beneath. The mortar in the bricks began to sprout poisonous black growths that bloomed and died.

Karmola invoked Two-Voice next. *"Maq keha moga nsu temk rsi."* Her words would latch on to nearby newly dead organic life and make them into twisted creatures that would attack at her command. A costly spell—Althus noticed how Karmola fought to not clutch her throat, but they needed this.

And Sajime had provided them with plenty of material to work with.

Hundreds of the sprouts shot out of the mortar like arrows and spun high into the air. The shop crumbled, startling the citizens of Messar into a rising chorus of screams, as Althus and the others made for the Eye of Messar. The sprouts transformed in mid-air into many-tendrilled birds of prey. The imperial agents that had been hiding amongst the crowd threw off their disguises and worked to attack Karmola's beasts. But the birds swooped through the air, snatching those that threatened them and ripping them apart with those flailing limbs.

The lobby was pandemonium. Everyone was scrambling away from the doors as more people poured inside. The screech of Karmola's monsters echoed through the walls. She looked pale. "It's okay. They're unruly, but I have a handle on them."

"Thought everyone was just going to flow where we needed them to be," Sajime said, sarcasm dripping from every word.

"The right ones will," Vade said.

Althus blinked at him, confused by a smile that didn't belong to the man he loved.

But the demon was too fast for him. *"Frin eena zeda."*

Althus couldn't move. He couldn't speak. In his mind, he desperately screamed out for Vade, but the demon was already gone. Althus knew this spell wouldn't last long, but too much could happen by the time it wore off.

*Too many humans in one place tends to do that.* He *knew* that hadn't sounded like Vade. But he had been too mired in his own outrage and anger to follow it through.

The demon had played them. No, Althus played himself.

# MESSAR — THE OPAL CONFERENCE

V ADE WAS TRAPPED behind the walls of his own mind while the demon guided his body like a puppet alongside the Phantom Dragons as they approached the dome. The twisted creature had spent years with Vade. He knew exactly how to imitate him; not even Althus noticed the difference. That stung more than Vade would have liked to admit.

*Maybe he doesn't love you as much as you think. Or maybe he doesn't know the real you at all. You spent so much time lying to him.*

Vade felt the demon drawing on his knowledge of the Eye of Messar's layout. One of the courtesans at Elayne's Gate had manipulated a client with a very useful kink into providing the Phantom Dragons a map. The dome-like building was divided by three hallways around a half-circle lobby, all of them leading to the Eye at its center, where Karmola's distraction was meant to drive everyone. They had intended to take the center hallway, clear out the six smaller conference rooms leading up to The Eye, and then wreak havoc.

The demon diverted and took the left hallway. Every step echoed beneath the gold-tinted glass ceiling. The overwrought opulence and excess screamed frailty to the demon. The torture dimension had never housed such weak, beautiful things.

*I can tear it down. You don't have to do this. You don't have to do anything but watch. Let me be the one.* Vade tried to plead with the demon.

The demon knocked over a grotesque sculpture of a large eye riddled with smaller ones like pus bumps. "The problem is, you think you understand me. You think you know the limits of my imagination. You have only scratched the surface of my world."

Vade felt everything that was happening—every step, every movement of his fingers, even the narrowing of his eyes. He simply had no control.

The demon moved Vade's lips in a smile, delighting in the misery. They walked down a curving hallway until they reached a small meeting room, where bureaucrats crouched beneath a table covered in papers. The green suits and skirts meant these were Phobeta Court officials, administrators, no one of real note. Their anger fascinated the demon. He regarded them the way Vade might stare at a good meal. Vade didn't understand it.

*How unimaginative of you! Especially when you're currently providing me such a feast.*

At that moment, Vade felt it. The demon was draining him. More than it ever had before.

*You want to be rid of me. But what if I get rid of you first?*

The bastard.

The Phobetans felt the malice flowing off the demon. They whimpered and closed their eyes, tears streaming at what they must have assumed to be their end. Vade knew they were right.

"Weakness. If you can't appreciate the glory in front of you then you don't deserve to see anything else."

The demon smirked and uttered something in Two-Voice so fast that Vade once again had no way of deciphering it. No Whisper spoke with such speed.

Horror overtook him as the first spasms of pain set in. Why could he feel their pain? That wasn't—

*A gift, Vade. You should know what this power you've so vagrantly flaunted does.*

The people screamed and writhed as their eyes began to bubble with unnatural heat. Vade could feel their agony as their eyes melted into a thick, viscous goo that dripped down their cheeks as their bodies jerked and contorted.

The demon sighed in pleasure. "Now come, Vade. They were hardly important to begin with."

These were enemies, but they didn't deserve that. No one did.

*Oh, plenty of people do. How insipid that you muster such empathy now when your whole life has been bereft of it.*

Vade had never reveled in the destruction of those opposed to him. It'd been a job—a *duty*—to stop those who worked against the aims of the Amos-Morbine Compact. And after, he certainly hadn't licked his lips like he'd just enjoyed an appetizing dinner.

*I'm sure your lack of joy in the killing is comforting to the dead.*

Vade didn't respond.

Their screams had attracted attention. As they stepped out of the gore-riddled room, Blacknails waited for them. Six in number, they wore black-plated armor with spiky shoulders that left their arms exposed. The veins on their hands were already bulging and glowing, the effect crawling up their arms. But when they saw that just one man had been responsible for all that death, the Blacknails took a step back almost in unison.

The demon clucked his tongue. "Cowards. But at least you appreciate what stands before you." He took a step forward, hands behind his back. "Your doom awaits."

Even if Vade could have told them to run, they wouldn't have listened. These were trained soldiers and they weren't about to abandon their duty now. The Blacknails drew their wooden swords. In the hands of anyone else, they'd be a joke, but summoned power surged through the unassuming weapons.

The swords blackened and lengthened as red pustules grew along the flat of their blades and the air grew thick with the scent of burning trees.Vade knew these soldiers stood no chance against the demon even if part of him hoped they could.

*You wound me Vade. Hasn't our collaboration been amusing so far?*

Sick bastard.

The Blacknails moved with predatory speed, surrounding the demon like a pack of lions. Their cuts came just as quickly, slicing into his shoulders and even lopping off two of his fingers, then cutting clear through the tendons in the back of one leg. The demon fell to his knees—Vade's knees—and Vade felt it all. For a moment, he thought maybe the Blacknails would win.

Then the demon laughed—deep, rich and powerful.

"An interesting magic. Though its wielders are lacking." He deflected another sword coming for his face with his bare hand, the sword cutting another wound across his palm. But then the demon spoke again, even faster than before.

The Blacknails screamed and dropped their swords— the flesh and muscle of their arms *peeled*, off and away from them. Blood and tissue slopped to the ground, pulled jerkily towards the demon, being absorbed into Vade's skin. The absorbed sinew scattered like ants and moved across the damaged parts of his body, knitting his fingers and tendons back together like a colony fiercely at work.

*You complained of fatigue. Consider this a gift.*

"The traitor lives after all."

The demon turned. It was Tiangu, the Peak from the Onyx Cabin, Desiree's prototype. Her proof that the Amos-Morbine Compact would rise above all others, with her at the helm. Vade felt oddly grateful—if there was anyone that could put a stop to his demon then it was someone with a bunch more stuffed inside him. There might even be a chance for Althus to get out of this safe. The best scenario would be the Peak and the demon destroying one another.

*Don't yearn for death so much. It doesn't suit you. And Desiree understands so little.*

"How long has she trapped my brethren in you?" the demon asked the Peak. Vade almost felt for the man with how casually disgusted the gaze was. "We are not made to exist in community, let alone be confined in one puny mind. Do you feel yourself getting angering? Are your words harder to come by? It's a common danger for those of us who linger too long in each other's company."

Tiangu sneered at the demon's inquiries. Vade wasn't surprised. The man was a Whisper and whatever sadism had seeped into him, Desiree's training wasn't something easily shaken.

*"Bru eada thix." "Niqu ghar't."*

The Peak blanketed the entire hallway in shadow and exhaled a cloud of noxious orange gas from his mouth, flying like a geyser towards Vade and his demon. The demon held his breath and side-stepped, the edges of the blooming cloud burning off Vade's shirt at the shoulder. Vade's flesh sizzled and he sincerely wished that the demon would stop being so reckless with his body.

*I thought you were after death? You must learn to be consistent.* He could punch the bastard.

*"Icazi'e."* Then: *"Filuh sto."*

Tiangu's words echoed from the dark, but the demon hadn't countered any of it yet. Vade wondered why. It couldn't mean anything good for their opponent.

The demon ducked away from a gigantic fist covered in ice, letting the Peak tumble over them, before slamming a hand into the man's stomach and speaking a rapid phrase in Two-Voice. He used Tiangu's momentum to flip him over and smack him into the tiled floor. The demon dusted his hands and spoke again, banishing the shadows. Darkness flecked away like pieces of rust from iron until the hallway was restored.

Tiangu writhed. The demon crouched as the Peak rolled around in agony. Tiny, white worms wriggled from his orifices. "You are an insult. Your kind fumbles through my world like drunk, vomiting children and somehow interprets it as excellence. That witless woman actually thought you magnificent!"

The demon plucked a worm from the Tiangu's lips. The squirming insect reeked of rotten eggs, its body lined with tiny barbs. "For millennia we stood alone and you think to trap us like zoo specimens to be used in your infinitesimally petty politics. I hope your pain is terrible and exquisite for my brethren who deserved far better than to die with you."

The Peak couldn't even scream as the demon enjoyed his agony. Vade almost trembled, knowing that if he died, the demon would go with him.

*Only if I'm not the one to kill you. And I find you and your lover intriguing. The bondage has had its...pleasures. But yes, I would rather be home and free.*

They left the remains of the Peak behind, just a mass of ripped flesh and viscera, now food for the white worms eagerly feasting upon him. All the bravado he witnessed at the Onyx Cabin had been undone in an instant. Had Tiangu ever stood a chance?

*No. None of them do. It's quite time they realize that.*

The empty hallway stretched before them, screams ringing in the distance. Too far away to tell if any of them belonged to the Phantom Dragons. Vade hoped not.

How many Peaks had Desiree brought? They could be fighting for their lives.

*Then we should go help them, shouldn't we?*

A grand flight of stairs led to the massive doors between them and the Eye. The stairs were painted with illustrations of a burning woman, a mockery of Chesyrah. A clear statement of where they stood on the fair distribution of power. If all was going according to plan, inside the Phantom Dragons were eliminating the cloistered servants of empire.

"You really have let Althus change you," the demon said as it swung open the grand doors.

Inside the Eye, none of the imperials knew that rebels walked among them. That they were the cause of the Opal Conference's disruption. It was admirable work. The layout of the central room made it easy to hide. Ornate white and brown tables with bejeweled chairs were scattered across the large circular floor, where people tried to create some semblance of fortification against the outside threat. Vade knew the place was once a concert hall.

"And your friends have made it a killing field." The demon cracked his knuckles. "Now this is when the fun starts."

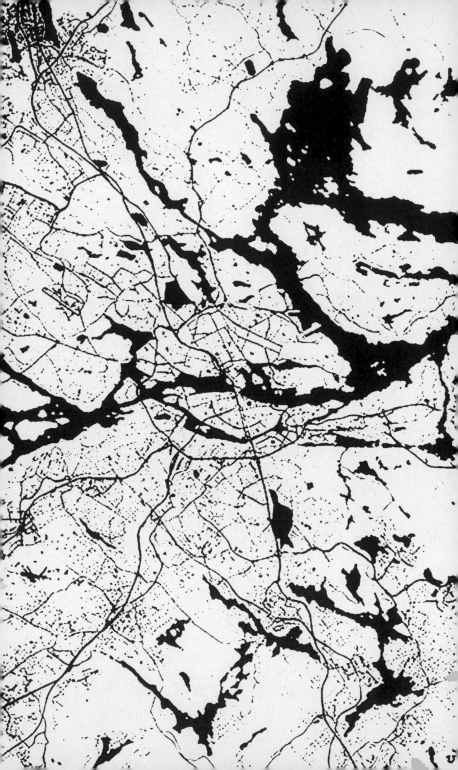

# MESSAR — THE OPAL CONFERENCE

THE PHANTOM DRAGONS had managed to turn the
Eye into pure pandemonium. Sajime had filled the
bureaucrats' lungs with spores that fed on emotion,
while Karmola stoked the paranoia amidst the chaos and
Althus barred the doors shut. Her Luminous Natalis VI
kept her black-smeared lips puckered at President Koo,
who only returned her intensity. Their retinues died
around them, clutching at their throats and falling to the
ground scratching at contaminated flesh, but still those
two refused to look away from each other, each convinced
the other was responsible for the attack. And as long as
neither died, that conviction became only more solidified.

Vade's gift of disguise allowed Althus and the Phantom
Dragons to appear like the other imperial bureaucrats. They
sliped in, sowed their chaos, and acted like they were victims
of it. They hid behind overturned tables and pretended
to tremble. They spoke frantically with security and then
switched to indignation when they didn't like the answers.

The three of them darted back and forth amongst the
dying, crushing windpipes while pretending to help. Althus
watched Sajime mimic the suffering of her own spores to
draw attention away from herself. He could practically
feel the glee coming off Karmola. They all had more than
enough reasons to hate these people, but she relished this
carnage in particular.

Althus buried any sympathy he might feel. These
people had been part of the suffering of millions and
regularly shrugged it off as a necessity of politics. Let them
cower behind tables and chairs, let their screams echo off
the high ceilings, let their blood and viscera twisted by
Sajime's magic seep into the floor. They had earned this
fate. He just wished—

For one cold moment, Althus couldn't think. He
didn't know where he was or *who* he was, then it all
came rushing back. The lack of knowing rattled him,
but the feeling reminded him of when he bonded with
Vade's memories. Had something happened to Vade?
Connecting with him so suddenly must mean—

"Althus!" The demon wearing Vade's skin had entered
the Eye. "I know you felt that too." It clasped its hands
together. "You and Vade are such a tragically hopeless
pair. Both dying for connection and not willing to let it
happen through me."

Althus froze. The Phantom Dragons had so far been
able to execute this without being noticed, but the demon
could expose them. *Would* expose them, if its sadistic
streak was anything to go by. They were past the point of
trying to get the demon to just leave.

Sajime had given him an idea back in Vazaba:

*"There are hundreds of languages in the world, right? And they're
always changing, they're always evolving over time,"* she'd said.
*"And if the demon's soul is—"*

*"—pure language, then we could change it."* Althus's eyes had
widened. *"Or change the meaning behind it entirely."*

*Sajime's grin had stretched from ear to ear. "You're gonna have to evolve Two-Voice."*

Althus's Two-Voice was something he learned from a more intuitive and less instructive place than Vade. He'd always had slightly unusual phrasings, ones that Karmola couldn't replicate. If Sajime's theory held up, in its own plane the demon was made up of pure language. A living expression of Two-Voice. Nothing more than one long monstrous string of words. Words that could be *spoken*.

And words carried the meaning that a speaker gave to them. So maybe he could change the demon's very definition.

As it finished prancing down the stairs and reached his side, the only thing Althus could think about was tearing it out of Vade and setting him free. But before he could test the words bubbling up within him, the demon shoved him away from a fireball flying inches from his face, close enough to singe his beard. Turning, he saw one of Desiree's Peaks. Fuck.

Altruism had nothing to do with why the demon had saved him, so now he was dealing with two enemies. He didn't know which to tackle first, but the question answered itself as a swarm of gray chittering bugs blanketed the demon, drawn up by Sajime from the fungal dead. She'd planned on calling those up later to dispose of any stragglers, but that card had gotten pulled early.

Sajime's skin crawled with pulsating green veins. "Stay away from him!"

*"Biandi'g."* Karmola used Two-Voice to make the bugs grow from small nuisances to a clambering pile of monsters that chomped and tore at the demon.

He knew it was necessary but Althus felt sick at the damage to Vade's body. This wasn't how things should end between them, but it was necessary. One other thing was sure now too: the demon had completely blown their plan of blending in. He could already feel the eyes focusing on them.

"*Keyadun tamagg!*" The complicated syllables flowed out like silk. A gamble on Althus's part; he'd often struggled with this phrasing. The connection with Vade gave him new confidence.

The Peak stopped short, as if he'd run into a wall, then stumbled backwards. Time around him had slowed and every step would feel like moving through thick sap. It wouldn't last for long, but Althus had brought himself some time.

But the bugs screeched, became solid rock and then crumbled to ash. Beneath them, Vade's suit had been torn to shreds, along with his shirt. Purple light gleamed beneath the muscles of his chest, but he looked otherwise unharmed. Dread and relief both roiled in Althus.

Vade came towards him. "Baby, it's me." Many in the crowd fled towards the doors.

Love made Althus want to believe. "Vade?"

Love also made him distracted. The Peak had pulled himself back up. He rushed Althus and backhanded him so hard Althus fell to the floor. A kick to the ribs kept him on the ground.

"He belongs to me!" Ice white lightning ripped from the demon's fingertips. Althus knew he had spoken Two-Voice again, but too quickly for him to understand. The lightning struck the Peak square in the chest. He hit the ground, convulsing and screaming.

Althus gritted his teeth and tried to stand, but the Peak had fucked him up. The chaos had stirred a morbid curiosity that Althus expected would become anger. The demon had exposed them. Desiree's new toy was a pile of melted flesh and bone. The demon grinned far too wide at the results of its work.

This might be Althus's only chance. He loved Vade, but this kind of horror had to end here. "*Ey——*"

"Ungrateful!" The demon's Two-Voice made Althus' mouth slam shut, his own words smothered. It crossed the space between them and kicked Althus even harder than the Peak had. "I make your little massacre *easy* and you *attack* me."

Despair fell over Althus. Had the world really given him this love only to pull it back in the cruelest way possible? But Althus's whole life had been about doing what he needed to survive. He didn't intend to stop now, even if it made him want to puke. "I thought you loved me."

The demon tilted his head to the side and bent down. "Of course I do. But respect has to be earned. You're going to be mine for a very long time. Rules must be established."

The demon kissed him hungrily, and Althus returned its passion, even though he despised it. If he kept it close maybe he could—

"Wait here. I'm going to dispense with these ridiculous pests."

Althus struggled to his feet with a groan as the demon approached the last of the Eye's survivors, where Desiree and her small guard surrounded President Koo.

"Vade! You bastard!" A small cadre gathered behind Desiree. Agents of the Enoch Consortius and the Phobeta Courts kept step with her. Somehow she'd managed to get them to stop bickering.

The demon grinned and held out his arms like he was ready to greet an old friend. "Desiree! I'm in awe. Child torturer, ruthless experimenter and arrogant horror. You continuously set the standard for your species."

"Kill this traitor."

The demon scoffed and rolled his shoulders back. "And we were just getting to know each other—"

"No! She's mine!" Karmola yelled. *"Drajar agiss ona sci iriga cla ean ndazu dega vola urg!"*

The air vibrated and shook the entire Eye as a shimmering purple wound shredded the air. Roars echoed from within, loud enough to make you piss yourself, just as a dragon erupted from the gash.

A translucent beast tore through the remaining attendees of the Opal Conference, its ghostly bites and flames tearing

at the souls of ignorant bureaucrats, cruel politicians, and
loyal soldiers alike. It destroyed them all the same and left
their minds husks. And more importantly, its swirling body
cut off anyone from getting to Desiree before Karmola.

She marched right up to a lone Desiree, using Two-Voice
to freeze her in place. Karnmols snatched the woman up
by her collar and pulled her close. "For Abel. For Cyn. For
every fucking kid you took from their homes."

The dragon roared one last time and smashed into
Desiree. She screamed and rattled, Karmola refusing
to let go even as blood and spittle oozed out of Desiree's
mouth. The dragon roared again and returned to the
torture dimension, the portal closing behind it. Desiree's
body slumped, her eyes completely vacant.

Karmola laughed, loud and heady.

But she barely had time to enjoy the victory. Althus
tried to warn her, but they were too fast—a Peak breathed
a geyser of green flame and Karmola fell back, protecting
her face with her hands, but the other Peak moved like a
blur behind her. Althus knew what was coming. Felt the
pain right in his stomach, but the foresight only made his
soundless scream worse.

The Peak grabbed her by the hair and slammed her
into the ground. Her knees folded awkwardly; her skull
cracked. Althus sprinted forward. She deserved to survive
this. Years of fighting couldn't end like this. It wasn't fair.

But end it did. The Peak brought his boot down and made
her head a violent, tragic mess of flesh, bone and blood.

Before he could reach her, Sajime tackled him to the ground.

"You can't! You can't!" Sajime's voice broke. "She's
gone! I can't lose you too."

The rawness there was enough to pull Althus out of his
blind rage. Althus gripped Sajime's arm, desperate for an
anchor.

Akjo. Taigan. Now Karmola. What hadn't Althus lost
in trying to keep Vade?

"This is not your fault," Sajime said. She always could read him. "You can't take on that burden, especially now."

She was right of course. Karmola's own words from years ago rang in his head too painfully clear; *grief never performed a single resurrection.*

The remaining Peaks were focused on protecting President Koo and Her Luminous Natalis VI. Their attention was on the demon. In better days, Althus might have been insulted by the dismissal. Now he just wondered how quick they were all going to die.

"Enough."

The demon's Two-Voice was still too fast for Althus to track it. The soldiers' lips just...melted off. They tore at their mouths as a buzzing filled the dome—only then did Althus take in how many people were affected. The buzzing was coming from inside them, their cheeks bulging and vibrating as creatures crawled inside of their bodies, unable to find escape. It seemed as if it had affected everyone remaining in the Eye but him. He hated these people and what they represented, but watching them die like this...

No! Sajime!

She stared at him, frantically clutching at her face.

Althus refused to lose her too. Not like this. It pushed him over the edge. Words. Language. Life was just how you found ways to communicate to each other. Poems. Stories. Sex. Souls crying out for connection. In his desperation, it all unfolded out for him.

He could see it now—the Two-Voice floating around everyone affected by the demon's power. Glyphs, runes, and words—they circled around each of them like finely spun tapestries. This was how he would change it.

Cradling Sajime, he reached into the tapestry surrounding her and started speaking to it. He didn't know what he was saying at first, but he filled new phrases with his intent, until he could change the demon's Two-Voice, flip it back and reverse it. The words came from that,

words to undo the flow of meaning and communication.
The flesh of her mouth parted. Her body stopped rattling
and she stopped tearing at her face.

Althus slumped against her.

"I love you." He squeezed her hand. "Get out of here. I
have to end this."

She nodded, exhaustedly pulling herself up.

"*Rula'n.*" Energy surged through Althus' body.

Althus sprinted forward, covering the space between
him and the demon in seconds, new inflections forming in
his mind, strange vocabulary shifting on his tongue—

—only to be snatched up by a powerful hand and lifted
into the air. The demon laughed. "Vade screams and
screams when I toy with you."

At least Sajime had gotten away. She would keep the
Phantom Dragons alive. Althus struggled but the demon's
vise grip was inescapable.

"Fuck you!"

Sajime! Damn it…why hadn't she run?

The demon groaned and dropped him, trapped by
Sajime in a host of glowing, thick blue vines. They pulsated
rapidly and drained its power. Vade's flesh had become
completely gray, and vines worked their way into his
mouth, pressed against his eyes.

But whatever well Sajime drew her power from was
costing her. Her nails had grown up and around, wrapping
around her forearms like bracers. Bloody cracks seeped all
over her skin. Her hair had completely fallen out.

"*Salah vi ehku er!*" A new phrase. It welled up from
within him, knowledge found through desperation. Althus
scrambled to his feet, doing everything he could to feed
Sajime the power she needed to really end this. Her vines
pulsed harder, as Vade's muscles atrophied and died.

But the demon spoke again.

The Eye shook, the ceiling cracking and falling. The
ground broke beneath them as Sajime screamed.

Althus watched helplessly as she was thrown backwards. She had pushed herself too far—her body crumpling like paper as she careened through the air, consumed by her power. What was left began to fold in on itself, spraying green and black poison.

This was the end, wasn't it? "I love you," he mouthed to that demon wearing Vade like a cheap suit.

He had lost too much. And he was running out of time. *"Come balik ckur! Break fruna eeloy!"*

The demon doubled over and gripped his stomach. "Seriously? I expected—" It scowled, unable to rise. "No. That's not. NO!"

Vade's voice broke through. "It's not enough, Althus. I'm not strong enough to hold him! You have to run!"

Althus tackled the demon to the ground. "Not a fucking chance!" He gripped Vade's face, desperation driving him. Language was its soul and a soul was a difficult thing to destroy. But if it could be weakened, made to break— Vade didn't need to do this alone.

*"Deyar moski'n must brum eadi'k!"* Althus's ears popped and blood ran down his nose. Two-Voice was a ball of yarn unraveling inside of him, re-shaping itself into something new. A power not born of torture, but something a demon couldn't understand.

The demon buckled and screamed as the symphony of buzzing mouths came to an end. Relief poured into Althus, but just as he saw Vade's smile break through, his own world went black.

# THREE WEEKS LATER — ABERNA

**V**ADE WIPED DOWN Althus's sweat-drenched forehead with a towel, kissed his cheek, and sat beside his bed to read. He'd been researching maps, testimonies, and carceral records illustrating how the Amos-Morbine Compact's military base bidding system had contributed to the increase in the practice of utilizing child soldiers across the world. Vassal nations competing for a chance to host a Compact base within their borders needed to prove how well they could assure said base's security—and the Compact turned a blind eye to how that security was procured. It wasn't easy subject matter, but he owed it to Althus to understand this history. At least many of the books were written in Kohi, a pleasant reminder of Olderiane.

Every day, the chaos of the Opal Conference felt more and more like an awful memory, while the calm of Aberna's mountainous jungle seeped into him. The fog in these warm mountains made it seem like clouds came to their cave to take a nice sabbatical from the sun's light. Vade didn't appreciate the oppressive humidity, but he adapted.

They had everything they needed in her: a bed
(honestly more a mattress supported by sticks), a one-
pot stove, and clean water. Aberna was far enough from
Messar that the locals hadn't asked many questions. The
few Compact accounts he had left contained enough buy
their silence for as they needed. Vade couldn't quite get
the cooking thing down, but only one of them was able
to actually taste the food he made. He gave Althus water,
spoonfed him when he could keep food down, and used
Two-Voice to keep his body going the rest of the time.

A loud, whooping howl echoed through the cave, met by
a group of hoots and then more howls. The jungle's silver-
eye monkeys and sun owls called out to each other, signaling
the start of a new day. It gave him hope that the pains of
yesterday could be soothed by the joyful noise of the present.
Vade had made up many stories about them and their long
and ancient rivalry about who could wake up first.

*Terrible creatures…terrible. If only they could resolve their differences…*

He put down his book and drifted to the cave entrance to
listen. Reading sometimes made his mind drift. It was hard
not to link the horrors in these pages to what he had seen
only weeks ago, and didn't take much for carnage to flicker
through his mind. The melting mouths, the boiling blood,
the bones growing inside bodies like weeds…they all crashed
against the shores of his thoughts and made his hands
tremble.

"Steady," Vade told himself. Better days. Just remember
better days. It was worth it.

Soon, Althus would wake up and they would make a
happy life for themselves. Their story didn't end in this
cave. It couldn't.

A dull, broken but familiar voice buzzed in the back of
his head. *End? Please. Yes, please end.*

Ever since Althus managed that new feat of Two-Voice,
the demon seemed broken. Like it couldn't quite form a

coherent thought. Vade suspected he would still be able to draw on some of the demon's power—there were words he'd never known stirring in the back of his head—but he hadn't yet. He was too afraid.

Amidst the call and response, Vade heard the smallest rustling. He hesitated to investigate—he didn't want to hope…but when silver-eye monkeys and sun owls finally brought their feud to an end, he heard it again.

"Vade? What's…what's going on?"

Elation radiated through him and made Vade's hands tingle. He couldn't remember the last time he'd been struck by such raw, unfettered joy.

He reached Althus's side so fast it almost felt like the moment didn't even happen. "I knew you'd come back. I knew it! You're too damn stubborn."

Althus cracked a weak smile. "Where'd I even go?"

Vade's breath caught. Where to even start?

But Althus's eyes lit up. "Never mind. I hear him in my head. I split him." He moved his tongue around his cheeks and across his lips, looking for moisture.

Vade got him some water. All the tiny, dark thoughts fighting for purchase in his mind were now ash on the wind. Hope flooded his heart in a torrent.

But Althus closed his eyes tight. "They're all gone."

Vade wished he could deny it. He turned away, not able to bear the pain on his lover's face. It was true. The Phantom Dragons were gone.

"I didn't bury them yet, but they're safe. I wanted you to make that decision." It was the least Vade could offer him. "Did they have families? Friends we should contact?"

Althus shook his head. "We all agreed when we went out, nobody knows. Telling the people we love that we're gone only puts them in danger. You confront death alone no matter what anyway. But the empires…what's happening? Tell me."

So Vade told him.

The empires were at each other's throats. Their leaders had been slain and the resulting struggles for power were the only thing keeping them from warring with one another, but it was only a matter of time.

"No one seems to know yet about the Phantom Dragons," Vade said. "I've sent dossiers to the Cotati Legion and other rebel groups I know, telling them what happened at the Opal Conference. I might have exaggerated a few details. The best propaganda tells a story people want to believe. And—it's working. The Phobeta Courts can barely keep a handle on their markets, and the Consortius's militia is in shambles."

Althus closed his eyes and took a deep breath. "We should—"

Vade closed the space between them and kissed Althus. For a moment, he felt like the kiss might not be returned until Althus held the back of his head, and Vade relaxed: some spark still existed between them. The kiss lasted too long and not long enough.

"Don't know how much longer I could have waited."

Althus laughed. "Was just waiting on you."

Vade rested his head against Althus' stomach and enjoyed the quiet rise and fall as he breathed. After a time, he felt a hand stroke his head and nearly cried. A moment like this felt almost impossible just a short while ago.

"So you…split the demon." Vade lifted his head to look at Althus. "What does that mean for us?"

"I learned to speak in a way it couldn't. Like any language, Two-Voice can become something different over time. Communication is a need more than anything else. And when I truly needed to find a way to reach out to you, I made language that allowed me to take part of the demon into myself and split its vocabulary between us."

*Silence. Please…silence.*

This felt like untouched territory. Vade knew they'd have to be more careful than ever with their magic going forward.

"You always manage the impossible."

"What's next?" Althus asked.

"Well, I've been thinking about it," Vade said. "The Phantom Dragons need to live on. If you're up for it, we don't stop."

"We?" Althus asked, cautious optimism in his tone. "Are you sure about that? Being a rebel and all?"

"Of course," Vade said, taking his hand again. "We take what we know about how the empires do things, and we do more damage. And I know Sajime would hate it, but I was hoping you could give me a tattoo like yours."

Althus laughed. "That's all the reason I need to do it!"

But just as soon as the laugh faded, he turned somber. "You're right. This isn't over. And I'm up for it. The empires need to answer for their crimes."

Vade squeezed his hand. "But first, there's somewhere I want to take you."

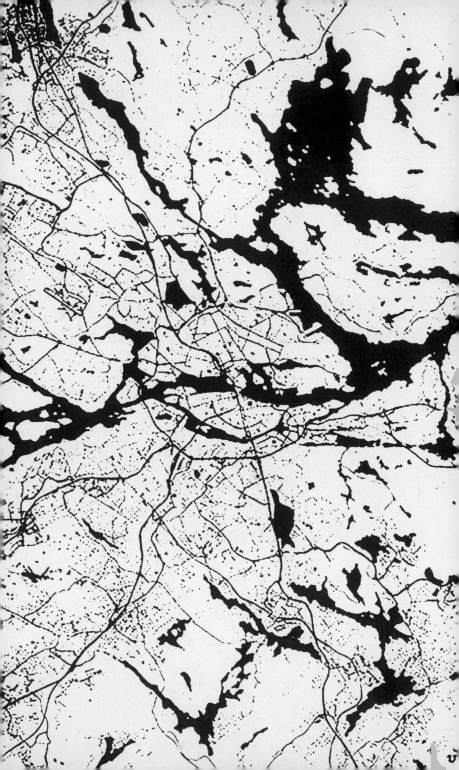

# EPILOGUE

## THE CORRIN ISLANDS — LAPIS BEACH

LAPIS BEACH HADN'T changed. Given everything happening in the world, Althus wasn't sure how long that would last, but for now, he closed his eyes and let the water lap against his skin. The balmy air caressed his naked body as he laid back on the sand.

The urn holding the combined ashes of the Phantom Dragons had been emptied and his friends were now one with the ocean. They had given everything for him. He never wanted them to, but they never stopped protecting him.

The tattoo on his arm was a reminder of both what he'd lost and what he'd gained. Vade had one now too, but it had been made with traditional ink and not a combination of dimensional powers. It would have to do for now, even if he knew how much Karmola and Sajime would balk at the idea.

Vade wasn't far away. The man had been hovering over him constantly since he woke up, and while it felt nice to have someone want him so intensely and honestly, Althus was glad to have a moment to himself. Besides, there was still a pleasure in watching Vade from afar: now he leaned up against the thin wood counter in front of the pop-up beach bar, getting another round of drinks. His time in Aberna had made his body even more lean and muscular. Sweat rolling down his back glistened in the sun. He was laughing and cracking jokes. After all the paranoia, it was nice seeing him let go of the constant vigilance.

The world had cracked at the seam and they slipped right through it, just like Vade said they could. The Amos-Morbine Compact lay on the verge of civil chaos from the power vacuum created after the conference. The Enoch Consortius and the Phobeta Courts were posturing at war, each blaming the other for the massacre. Many of the smaller nations pled for peace, but their proxies couldn't do much to stem the tide. And the most prominent international news outlets predicted crisis after crisis by the end of the year.

But a crisis for the empires was an opportunity for the Phantom Dragons. Each one a sapling of change pushing through the ground. His people would have been happy with it, but it wasn't enough. A sapling could still be crushed underfoot. If he was going to make sure the others truly had a legacy worth remembering, then he had to push the imperials to ruin. His Two-Voice was stronger than ever before. The demon inside made him feel like he could fight a hundred Whispers if he needed to.

*No...no more...please quiet.*

Althus scoffed at the broken demon's command and locked it in the back of his mind with ease. The world was full of monsters, and maybe holding one without mercy made him one too, but Althus had no compunctions about thinking himself unsalvageable if it meant creating new hopes for those who need it most. He may have started to become resigned that he'd never see the smiles of Sajime and the others again, but he would never stop fighting for the dreams they'd forged together.

Althus smiled at the scene at the bar. More people now had drifted towards it, drawn in by Vade's magnetic charm. He still never had to be loud—he was just effortlessly captivating. Rolling back all his heavier thoughts, Althus inconspicuously walked through the crowd until he reached Vade's back. He let his fingers playfully brush against his lover's ass.

"You seem fun. Can I buy you a drink?"

Vade's grin was infectious and most of all, genuine. The two of them were finally getting to let their music play. Most of the trappings of their old games were gone forever, but they both had agreed to keep this one.

"I'd love that. Maybe we can get to know one another better."

O

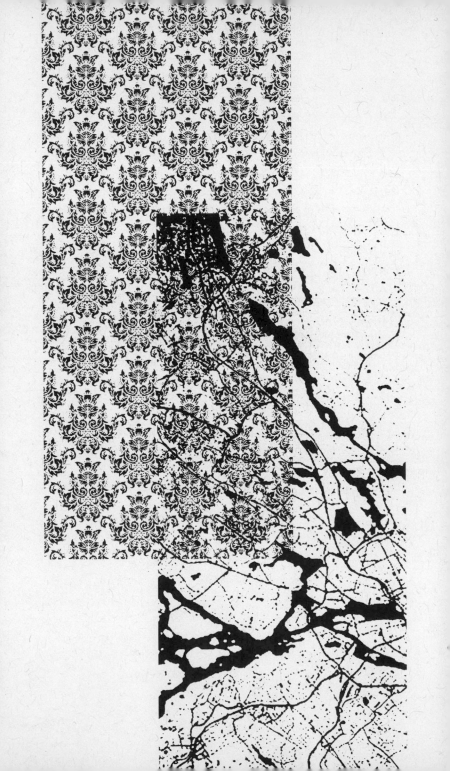

# ACKNOWLEDGEMENTS

NOTHING IS EVER really created in solitude. I am only here because of the many people who have never let me give up on myself. To my family: Mom, Dad, Lionel, Nastassia and Sharonda, you are my foundation. I exist as a writer because you all always let me. My friends that became family: Eyad, Chad, Maggie, Ricardo, Chris, Stephen, Bryan, Greg, Barry, Cierra and so many more—thank you for being my light guiding me through the tunnel and keeping me grounded through this whole process. Thank you for loving me for me. My writing angels: L.D. Lewis the mighty, Danny, Nia, Suzan, Bendi, Wendi and the writing group you cultivated, Shingai, DaVaun and more (because the SFF community overflows with great people), each of you saved me at different points in this process. The finish line would not have been obtainable without you. My Just Keep Writing podcast crew, you spoke life into me over and over again when I was not always feeling my best. Thank you is hardly enough. And Cathy Kwan, I will never ever forget the amazing cover you created for this book. Your talent is unparalleled!

Finally, and probably most importantly, thank you to dave and Neon Hemlock. Thank you for thinking I could do this. Thank you for being patient with me. Thank you for cheerleading me on. Thank you for pushing me to take the creative chances I didn't think I was ready to take. I'm a better writer and quite frankly, a stronger person because of this entire process. I could not have imagined a better partner for this book to enter the world with. I am honored because the work you do is so important and I will forever be thrilled that I got to be a part of it.

# About the Author

Brent Lambert is a storyteller, a dreamer and a hopeless romantic who happens to like alot of nerdy shit. He will never stop believing in the transformative power of speculative fiction across media formats. As a founding member of *FIYAH Literary Magazine*, he eventually found himself part of a Hugo Award winning team. He resides in San Diego but spent a lot of time moving around as a military brat. His family roots are in the Cajun country of Louisiana. Coming up, he will be part of the upcoming Black horror anthology *All These Sunken Souls*. Ask Brent his favorite members of the X-Men and you'll get different answers every time. Ask him his favorite Avatar and the answer is Kyoshi always!

# About the Press

Neon Hemlock is a Washington, DC-based small press publishing speculative fiction, rad zines and queer chapbooks. We punctuate our titles with oracle decks, occult ephemera and literary candles. Publishers Weekly once called us "the apex of queer speculative fiction publishing" and we're still beaming. Learn more about us at neonhemlock.com and on Twitter at @neonhemlock.